LOVED

A Novel

Kimberly Novosel

*****

An Inspivia, Incorporated *Company.*

This is a work of fiction. The names, characters, places and incidents are the product of the author's imagination or are used fictitiously. Any resemblance to actual events, locales, or persons, living or dead, is entirely coincidental.

Inspivia Books
Memphis, Tennessee, 38114
books.inspivia.com

LOVED: A Novel
© Copyright 2012 by Inspivia Books.
Editor - M. Brock
Author Photograph – Tim Hiber
Cover Designer – Holley Maher of H. Maher Creative
Book Illustrator – Holley Maher of H. Maher Creative

All rights reversed. No part of this book can be used or reproduced, in part or in whole, by any means, by anyone, without written permission from Kimberly Novosel or Inspivia Books.

For permission to reproduce the information in this book for commercial purposes or redistribution, please e-mail:
copyrights@inspivia.com

To contact the author, Kimberly Novosel:
loved@kimberlynovosel.com

ISBN-10: 0984845925
ISBN-13: 978-0984845927

LIBRARY OF CONGRESS CATALOGING-IN-PUBLICATION DATA
2012952333
Kimberly, Novosel
Loved/Kimberly—2012 Inspivia Books

This Inspivia Books Paperback Edition November 2012
Inspivia Books is a trademark of Inspivia, Inc.
Printed in the United States of America

For more information about this book and the author:
www.theoohlalalife.com

MORE TITLES *from* INSPIVIA BOOKS

BOUNTIFUL FAMINE – A NOVEL *by* SHEG ARANMOLATE
Bountiful Famine is an intriguing story of young Nadus, inspired by actual events in Africa's history and present. Readers from any background will still gain insight from what unfolds in this emotionally gripping journey that will entertain, enlighten, and astonish.

BEWARE OF OPEN WINDOWS *by* PHILIP ZYG
Never leave your windows open. Who knows what may pop in... or out. Flashes from an obscure, yet familiar reality where dead languages turn on TV sets and cats take off for outer space. Beware of Open Windows is a collection of over a hundred poems.

iACTUATE: *by* SHEG ARANMOLATE
iACTUATE: 100 days of Inspiration is a thought-provoking book that is filled with succinct stories, describing many life situations that remind readers that they can fulfill their desire to act on inspiration.

CONTENTS:

Zero:	1
One:	3
Two:	28
Three:	42
Four:	66
Five:	97
Six:	119
Seven:	147
Eight:	164
Nine:	178
Ten:	195
Eleven:	202
Twelve:	212
Thirteen:	231
Fourteen:	247
Fifteen:	261
Sixteen:	272
Seventeen:	293

To Heather, my anchor.

To Carrie, my compass.

For Chase, the ship.

"Well I guess you left me with some feathers in my hand.
Did it make it any easier to leave me where I stand?"

Counting Crows

PRESENT DAY:

I stood at the locked entrance to my storage unit this morning, the orange metal gate exactly the harsh color of traffic cones.

Caution.

I had a good idea of what I would find in there among the love letters and CD cases, in between my old pink flea market chair and Christmas decorations—all my past selves. I sighed as I resolved to dive in and get the job done. Before two hours were up, I had managed to get most of the boxes and furniture into the truck that I had rented for the occasion.

All that remained in the small rectangular room were a few litters of trash and one box that stood at my feet. Without further contemplation, I knew right then that the battered wooden box wasn't going into the back of the truck with the rest of the stuff, as I didn't have any room for it in my present life. Inside the container were books of all different shapes and sizes, some covered in satiny material, some covered in leather, a few colorful and some were simple. I picked one out of the pile and noticed that the way it fit in my hand was so natural like a surgeon with a ten blade or a piano player's fingers against the keys. After all the time that I had spent cradling each one, my hands should know them all so well; that's what they all shared in common—my handwriting and years and years worth of my words, from my hands, on my best days and my worst.

I slipped the book back into the box and in that moment I realized what I would do with them. As I was about to embark on a new chapter in life, there would be no better time to revisit those days and those past selves for one last time. I put the box next to me in the cab of the truck, ready, though apprehensive to relive my own story and to set it free. I would be in denial if I didn't appreciate the reality that everything in those journals has transformed me into the woman that I am today.

The truth, however, is that I'm not the only protagonist in this story. So are you. We're all challenged on a daily basis by the same things in life, written in similar words and painted from the same colors. Sometimes it's a burst of vivid purple, a broken heart struggling to breathe, and sometimes it's the deep inky blue of a dark hole, seemingly with no light at the end. Sometimes it's the intense red of anger born from a pattern of disappointment after disappointment or the fiery yellow of a lesson learned. On other days, it's the fresh

PRESENT DAY

green of a new triumph or the dull gray of a day lost to not knowing where to go next.

Today, I can say with a strong level of confidence that I know where I'm headed to next, and so I have decided to share my story with you because I believe that no matter how you wrote your story, it reads something like this.

This is how I became who I am.

So Far

It was my twentieth birthday. I was wearing my new red Betsey Johnson dress, my big blue eyes lined in black Kohl liner and an extra coat of mascara. Nashville's November was chilly but not the bone-crushing cold of Pennsylvania. I was sitting in an iron chair on the patio at Hamilton's, sipping a French martini. All around me couples were talking and touching hands. Groups of friends were laughing. I was alone.

I swirled the pink liquid in the almost-empty glass.

Time for a third, I thought.

Most of the people who had been my friends in my first two years at college were no longer my friends, by no fault of my own. Or was it? Anyone who was still considered my friend was supposed to be at that table with me.

Where are they?

As I finished my drink, I considered all the places I could be instead of alone at my own birthday party and with too much time to think about the last two years. I could be at my apartment, fast asleep in bed but I never got any sleep anymore. I could be at Ethan's, where there was sure to be more booze and who knew what else.

"Another drink, beautiful?" Joey always waited on me there, always called me "beautiful," and always served me drinks underage.

"Yes, please." I smiled briefly before returning to my train of thought.

How did I end up here, alone on my birthday?

Twenty, I thought. *Only twenty years old.*

I had already fallen so far.

1
Three Throws for a dollar

June, 1999.

"I knew you'd be out here all day so I brought you Wendy's. And I have some good news!"

I had just parked my very first car in the driveway of my very first boyfriend's house, where he and his stepdad were working to fix the car that his grandmother had given him. It was never running. He had to drive mine to prom a month earlier while his sat in my driveway, smoke billowing from the hood.

"Aw, thanks baby! We thought we had it fixed but then it wouldn't start again. What's the news?" He was tall but not strikingly so and strong, a soccer player, with dirty blonde hair and sparkling blue eyes. He was handsome but mostly nondescript. I handed him the Wendy's bag and he opened it and smelled the contents: double cheeseburger and large fries, his favorite.

"The owners of the Park gave me and Crystal a show! We're going to sing there this summer."

He threw his head back and laughed, and that's when I saw it. Clear as day, a round purple mark on the side of his neck about halfway between his collarbone and his jaw. My face burned red hot and suddenly everything moved in slow motion.

"What's that?" I asked, my voice coming out weak and my pulse suddenly audible, like a drum signifying danger in a movie scene. I lifted his chin with my fingertips hesitantly as if touching him might melt my skin. His expression changed from one of youthful mischief to one of panic, like when something horrible happens that you should have, but didn't, see coming.

I surely didn't see it coming.

"It's not what you think, Kim," he started. It was odd to hear his voice without its usual hint of humor in his tone. It took on a strange adultness.

"It's a hickey! I..." I shook my head. The word sounded dirty, foreign. "I don't even want to know. I'm...going. I'm...done." I turned and got in my car. He just stood there

ONE - THREE THROWS FOR A DOLLAR

and watched me go, clutching the greasy fast food bag in his hand.

I cried for a week, couldn't sleep, wouldn't eat. It was the first time in my life I had felt unwanted, rejected, knowing that someone had gotten to know me and then decided he didn't want to know me anymore. A hole had been ripped open in my chest, but as they say, the younger you are the quicker you heal.

This was my first broken heart.

I grew up in Westville, Pennsylvania, a small industrial town of dingy two-story buildings under a perpetually gray sky. My parents left Pittsburgh after getting married to start a business in Kettle Lake, near Westville, which, at the time, was a popular vacation spot for Pittsburghers. Many people owned cottages there and spent the summers on the lake in their pontoon boats or riding the old wooden rollercoaster at Kettle Lake Park, the lakeside amusement park that opened in 1890 and hasn't been updated since.

My parents, both from large Catholic families, had grown up in small, crowded houses where they wore hand-me-down clothes and ate their toast even if it was burnt as wasting wasn't allowed. Although they raised me with similar values, they also wanted to create a life where their children had more than they did, and we were taught to believe that we could accomplish anything and we could be anyone we wanted to be.

We lived on nearly a hundred acres of land where I would read books in the fields or crawl out of my window to lie in a nook in the roof and wonder at a sky full of stars. Every week we attended Mass at St. Joseph's Church. We prayed before meals. We didn't use swear words. My brother and I went to a Catholic school through the eighth grade, where we walked from class to class in a line with each student holding the door for the next. The same twenty-three kids were in my class for those nine years. My world was flipped when I enrolled in public high school, where throngs of strangers in their own choice of clothes rushed in all different directions between bells. Halfway through high school, I had almost but not quite figured out where I fit in.

My best friend Crystal lived in the farmhouse on our land with her mom and her mom's boyfriend. We were very different. She rode barrel horses and spit in the grass. She wore shirts short enough to show her tanned boyish belly, knew how to pluck her eyebrows and ran her fingers casually through her thick blonde hair. She said whatever she wanted to say and did pretty much whatever she wanted to do. Before I knew her she lived in Ohio, where she drank Jack Daniels and slept with cowboys.

ONE - THREE THROWS FOR A DOLLAR

It was our love of country music that tied us together. We spent most of our time hanging out in her room talking about boys and listening to Garth Brooks, Reba McEntire, and LeAnn Rimes. To be honest, it was probably our love of boys and country music that tied us together, though so far I had only had the one boyfriend.

Crystal got a summer job working at the karaoke stand on the midway at Kettle Lake Park. I would go hang out, sing with her and help get people excited to pay to sing karaoke. Mostly, people would stop to watch us sing and then move on to play skee-ball or ride the coaster or walk down to the little beach. The owners of the park were impressed with the crowds that would gather and we were thrilled when they asked us to perform a show a few times a week. We were singing along to tracks, but we loved it. We signed autographs for people who brought the clippings of our picture from the Westville Times, people who thought we were somebody. We hoped we would be someday. I didn't let it discourage me that some of the Westville kids were spreading rumors that we got our own show because we gave the park owners sexual favors. I hated to think anyone believed something about me that was so far from the truth. But for the first time in my life people were talking about me and I liked it.

I ran into my first ex-boyfriend once at the park with the girl who had given him the hickey. I heard they met in the Wal-Mart parking lot. I consoled myself by daydreaming that one day my CD would be on the shelves at Wal-Mart and he would be innocently walking past the music section and see my face. He would stop, his eyes would get huge as he picked it up off the display and he would then fall to his knees and cry.

Crystal and I went to see a big country music festival in Pittsburgh. It was a sweaty hot summer day with no clouds to provide relief from the sun. In short shorts and little tank tops we ran all over the festival, our faces reddening and our shoulders tanning, with stars in our eyes. Kenny Chesney, the Dixie Chicks and Tim McGraw were on the main stage but our attention was on a band of six brothers on a small side stage. They all played their own instruments—from dobro to mandolin—and they were all around our age. We watched their set until Crystal, with her full lips and big smiles and a mischievous look sparkling in her green eyes, caught one of the guys' attention and got us invited into the roped off area behind the stage.

While Crystal flirted with some of the band members, playing her giggle like a practiced instrument, I asked a million questions about touring and the music industry: Music Row, record labels, life on the road, no detail bored me. I couldn't wait to go on tour. Not as a singer, necessarily, but as a manager or something else exciting.

Eventually the guys said they had to go perform a song on the big stage and we should come with them.

"Put these on and you can come with us," one of them handed us stickers for our shirts.

"Oh, cool," Crystal said.

I added, "Thanks!"

Backstage passes! As we headed inside the stadium and past the security guards, we were both giddy but tried our best to act like this was something we did all the time: *Oh yeah, that's Tim McGraw singing "Don't Take the Girl" and here I am watching from the wings of the stage just like any day.* Inside, I couldn't believe I was twenty feet away from him as he performed the first country song I ever liked for a stadium full of people. I couldn't believe Faith Hill was to my right, holding her little girl and looking gorgeous in a leopard dress. And past her, the Dixie Chicks were waiting to go on stage. *Just like any day. In a dream!*

Crystal and I exchanged an *Oh my gosh!* glance.

I wasn't just any lucky fan backstage that day. This was like a field trip to me, like an independent study of music. I knew every country record that had come out in the last three years and the names of every writer and producer in Nashville. That day I started to think that maybe I had a chance to meet the right people, and I don't mean just the stars. I knew that the artists couldn't start my career in country music. It was the managers, record labels, production companies and so forth who I ought to be meeting. I also knew instinctively not to act like a fan. I didn't ask for autographs. I was very careful not to overstep my boundaries as far as getting phone numbers or hanging out too long after shows. I made an effort to come off as mature, interesting, and most importantly, professional.

 I watched Crystal use that special magic she had to get whatever she wanted. I studied her too: the way she pulled the audience in when we performed, the confidence she showed in the tilt of her head, the sway of her hips, how she made unbreakable eye contact with a guy when she was flirting with him—that dangerous spark growing brighter and brighter.

 As summer heated up, I found that Crystal and I weren't always where we told my parents we were or doing what we were supposed to be doing. Her mother wasn't around much so if we were home, we were at her house listening to music, watching movies I wasn't allowed to watch, or trying on the clothes that I had to sneak out of my house

ONE - THREE THROWS FOR A DOLLAR

because I wasn't allowed to lend them to her. I liked to wear her clothes too.

One night Crystal and I were hanging out by the tent that we had strategically placed so my parents couldn't see extra cars when she had guys come visit us at all hours of the night. Crystal was wearing sporty pants made of a cheap shiny lilac material and a very small white tank top. You could see her belly ring, one of her many piercings not put there by a professional, but by me and a sterilized safety pin. She had cut her long blonde hair into a pixie cut which she decorated with glittery bobby pins she stole from Wal-Mart.

The last corner of sky had turned black and the crickets sang as if their day had just begun. I was holding one of my kittens and Crystal was texting some guys from her cell phone. She wanted Trey to come over. He was one of the popular guys in her class and a year older than me. I thought he had a girlfriend but he had been hanging out with Crystal lately. I noticed that most of the guys who hung out with Crystal acted like they didn't know her when they saw her elsewhere. Trey answered Crystal's text, letting her know that he would be over soon. Crystal's eyes began to gleam that satisfied sparkle I was getting to know so well. She smiled mischievously, the dimple in her chin deepened and then she spat on the grass. She had taught me how to spit when we cleaned the barns.

"God, he's so hot," she said, clearly gearing up for an evening with Trey. "Don't you think so? I would have him bring a friend but..."

"No, that's ok," I interrupted, waving her off. I didn't need some random guy to keep me company. The last time she did that it was a guy from Ohio named Rooster who tried to kiss me in the barn. "I'll be fine on my own."

I thought about how very early in our friendship my parents had decided that Crystal made them uncomfortable. I knew why but I also thought that if she was nice enough to me, what did it matter what she did when I wasn't around? She didn't make me steal or drink so who cared? Perhaps, I explained to them, I might even be a positive influence on her. I even took her to youth group with me a couple times. Though, if I was honest with myself, she did make me uncomfortable sometimes too.

Trey pulled up in his red low rider truck. We all stood outside the tent and talked for a few minutes before going inside and zipping the doors shut. The ground was hard under my sleeping bag so I tossed around a few times trying to get comfortable while Crystal and Trey whispered. I wondered to myself if I should just go ahead and walk up the driveway and get a good night's sleep in my bed. Crystal giggled.

ONE - THREE THROWS FOR A DOLLAR

I tried to explain that I was going to head home but they both insisted I stay. I knew I would only make it worse if I argued. It would make me seem more childish. Instead, I put the pillow over my head and pretended I was somewhere else while they had sex in her sleeping bag next to me.

I believed that sex was special and here it was in front of me with no love story in sight. I knew that Crystal would pay no penance for her sins. She was doing what she wanted to do and she would get away with it. Then she'd do it again. I fell asleep feeling sad and confused; my own values suddenly were worth so much less in this strange new light.

For the rest of the summer, our days were spent singing or hanging out with guys at the park while our nights served as my introduction to a life of teenage rebellion; though I still felt more like a fly on the wall than a participant. Sure, I made out with a couple of guys who paid me a little bit of attention but I never let it go farther than kissing. I was worried about being thought of as a tease but I didn't see the point of going further with any of these boys. None of them seemed like boyfriend material to me and that was what I was after. What I had been through with my first boyfriend caused my hope in Westville guys to wane. Plus, I was setting my sights on a life in the music industry. Everything else was just temporary.

August, 1999.

My parents, Crystal and I drove about two hours south to see our new friends in the band of brothers play at the West Virginia State Fair. It was a much smaller production than the country festival so it was easy for us to find the guys before the show, no passes needed. We stood around the back of the stage where some of the brothers and their crewmembers, many of whom we'd met at the last show, were loading in their gear. We hadn't met their tour manager, Paul, a very tall guy with an oval face and wavy blonde hair covered with a black ball cap that read, "CAA."

I watched him as he messed with cords and instruments and instructed the others on what needed to be done next. He had a kind but authoritative tone, not bossy or cold, but definitely serious and responsible. Suddenly, he looked up at me from across the stage, straight into my eyes and grinned. The moment lasted long enough that I blushed. When he turned away, I said to Crystal in a low voice, "That's the guy I've been looking for. I'm going to marry him."

"I'm never getting married," she said, "but good for you."

We sat in the grass in front of the stage and watched the band play. I studied their reactions to each other and the comfort they had with their instruments. They'd been playing their whole lives and it showed. I lay back in the grass and listened as small clouds moved slowly across the sky. I could feel the warmth of the sun on my face despite the cool late-summer northern air. The music floated around me, through me; it was part of me. Crystal, my parents and everyone around me was enjoying the show, sure, but I thought I was experiencing the music in a very different way. This was my destiny, unfolding itself across the West Virginia grass and into my soul.

After the show, I talked with Paul outside the bus for a while about how he had come to work with the brothers and what Nashville was like. He asked about my ambitions and my hometown. We exchanged phone numbers and promised to stay in touch.

Just before school started Crystal showed her horses at our county fair, the social event of the summer. It was the first chance for everyone to see friends who'd scattered for the summer and a chance for me to run into Jeff Meyers. My crush on him was two years old, sparked when I sat behind him in freshman Algebra. I would detail for Meredith, my best friend in that class, every word he ever said to me. We would dissect his tone and vocabulary for any shred of interest on his part, but we knew that asking a girl if you can borrow her pencil is in no way a romantic gesture. Still, I hoped I would see him at the fair and that suddenly he would notice me and we could leave Westville together.

I stayed in the trailer with Crystal at the horse camp so that I could be at the fair every night. I met up with Meredith most of the time because Crystal hung out with the carnies and the cowboys and they made me nervous. Her school friends made me uncomfortable but I flat out didn't belong with her fair friends. Plus, I wanted to see some of the girls who I had been neglecting over the summer.

As I walked the midway with some friends from my class, I remembered my first concert, which was at this very fair. I was thirteen and so was LeAnn Rimes. In awe, I watched her and I knew that if she could be in the music business so could I.

I wandered the dusty paths between the throw-a-dart-at-the-balloon game and the squirt-the-water-in-the-hole game, ignoring the sounds.

"Hey there beautiful, does the pretty girl want to play? I'll give you three throws for a dollar. C'mon!"

I rolled my eyes. I knew better than to be flattered; they were supposed to say stuff like that. These guys were selling something. They weren't really seeing me, wanting to talk to me or calling me pretty.

And what would I win anyway? A plastic frog? A stuffed teddy bear? That frog won't turn into a prince and I

ONE - THREE THROWS FOR A DOLLAR

want something better than a teddy bear hugging me at night. No, my mind was far away, scanning the crowds of couples with stuffed tigers and kids with cotton candy, waiting for Jeff Meyers to appear and tell me he'd missed me all summer. Maybe I would give him that special look I was starting to learn. Meredith snapped me out of my daze and told me it was time we go home; summer was over for us this year.

September, 1999.

School started in the fall and I became increasingly eager to get out of Westville and start on the path to my future. I talked with Paul, the tour manager, on the phone most nights. It wasn't all business. In fact, it wasn't much business. He definitely flirted with me. My own phone line would ring right about the time I should have been going to bed and it was Paul calling from whatever town they were in that night. I would hide under the covers and talk quietly so my parents wouldn't know I was up so late, just like when I was a kid and would read books under the covers with a flashlight.

Our conversation spanned from talking about our church backgrounds to what I was sleeping in (boxers and a T-shirt), to what city they'd just played and where they were headed next (Indianapolis or maybe Wichita). He told me all about the people he had met on the road and about the unreleased albums he'd heard that he thought I might like. I told him about my theatre class and the bonfire parties we had at our house over the fall. When he was flirting, he spoke in a soft voice, like we were telling secrets. He would ask if I was dating anyone at school. I told him these guys didn't understand me. We both kept saying we looked forward to seeing each other again.

In one of our conversations, Paul told me about a school in Nashville called Belmont University where "Music Business" was one of the majors. I didn't even know such a thing existed.

"It's really well known and the program is great," he told me. "The students all do internships on Music Row," he added as if he even needed to sell it to me.

"That's amazing!" I whispered with excitement. "I have to go there!"

"You absolutely should and I wouldn't mind having you in Nashville," he said and I could hear the smile in his voice.

That is how I can make this happen! I didn't just have to dream it anymore. I knew the next step: College in Nashville, specifically to be an artist manager. I was starting to see a path for my future that began with escaping Westville. How soon can I go?

ONE - THREE THROWS FOR A DOLLAR

The thought of two more years in Westville made me want to die so I went to my guidance counselor and asked him if there was any way I could graduate early. He discovered a program called Early Admission, where I could attend Belmont as a full time freshman the following year and count any classes needed for high school towards my graduation at Westville. I would then graduate high school after my first year of college. It sounded too good to be true. If this was real, I could be at college orientation in a less than a year.

I went home and told my parents about it. Their first reaction was that I could go if it was only a semester early but not for the entire year. I argued. I pleaded. We met with the counselor and eventually they agreed that I could apply and if I got in, I could go.

December, 1999.

We flew to Nashville over Christmas break to visit Belmont University. My parents agreed that Crystal could tag along if she was responsible for herself and got her own hotel room. I barely even looked at the school. We saw the outside of the library and a few other buildings. We noticed the campus' proximity to Music Row. My feet hit the soil and I knew that it was where I belonged. Every brick was calling my name. I didn't care if it was early or not, it was the only place for me.

Paul drove Crystal and I around town. He took us to the brothers' apartment and a couple of the guys came with us to get coffee at a place called Café Coco. I liked Café Coco right away. There were a lot of young artistic-looking people hanging out there. I ordered something called a Café Loco, an iced coffee drink with banana flavor and it was delicious.

The sparks Paul and I had over the phone were definitely there in person. He always looked me in the eyes when he was talking to me and even when he wasn't. He hugged me a bit longer than if he was saying *hello* to an acquaintance. He spoke very highly of me and of my ambitious nature when he introduced me to his many friends. After coffee, he drove me back to my hotel then took Crystal to hers.

The next day, my family and Crystal went to see Tim McGraw and Faith Hill in concert to ring in the New Year, all breathing a sigh of relief when Y2K didn't cause the world to end. We also stopped at the Country Music Hall of Fame, where we admired old Dolly Parton costumes and took pictures on a pretend Opry stage, pretending to be singing into a pretend microphone.

But soon, it would all be real to me, all of my dreams! I was moving to Nashville, heading toward a career on Music Row. I was excited about the prospect of spending more time with Paul. He was a good friend to have or maybe more than a friend, I didn't know yet. Regardless, being around him made me happy and that was something to be excited about. Everything in my life seemed to be falling right into place.

Back in Westville, it was school, snow and boredom as usual. Crystal and I went out for pizza. She was talking about a rodeo that she was going to in Ohio the following weekend. I was only half-listening, thinking about my upcoming SAT's and trying to estimate the number of days before August. I took a bite of my cheese pizza, thinking it had to be something like 200 days, maybe 230, when she broke me out of my daydreaming.

"I have to tell you something," she giggled and bit her lower lip, the dimple in her chin deepened.

I was beginning to hate the moments when she was so pleased with herself for doing something I most likely didn't agree with and making light of things I took seriously. I was starting to resent how she would do anything to be the center of attention. I was becoming aware of how she would put me on the back burner when sex or alcohol was available to her. I knew I wasn't going to like what she was about to tell me.

"I slept with Paul."

She smiled proudly, her eyes gleamed but her words sank into my stomach like stones. That was the moment! That was the glass breaking. That was the beginning of the end. I blinked a few times at her and felt my chin begin to quiver and then my eyes spilled over with tears. I wanted out of there. I didn't want my pizza anymore; I wanted to throw it at her.

"I shouldn't have told you," she said, trying to brush it off. She took a big bite out of her pepperoni slice.

She thought she could have protected me by not telling me like I was some silly little girl. My mind was screaming. *Shouldn't have told me?! How about shouldn't have done it!* She knew how I felt about Paul, how rare that was for me and how important he was. I had no words. What I really wanted to say would have had no effect on her. It was beyond my vocabulary or my level of strength to make her understand who I thought she really was. I could call her all the names I wanted to but in the end, she would probably just smile and tell me it was sad that I didn't understand the world better—that I was so naïve.

So I didn't say anything at all.

I didn't say anything that day, the next day or the next week. We just stopped being friends. My eyes had been opened to her and my other friends and my parents were re-

ONE - THREE THROWS FOR A DOLLAR

lieved. Meredith and the girls, on the other hand, were so supportive of me and their values were more in line with mine, anyway, so I focused on spending more time with them.

Our split affected us in very different ways. Without Crystal pulling me down, I soared. Without me building her up, she sank. I quit seeing her in the halls at school and eventually I heard she'd dropped out.

I felt so powerful. I learned I could close my heart to someone. She no longer had any effect on me. I didn't have to wonder if I was cool enough or fun enough, I didn't have to fight all her boys for her attention or fight her for the attention of a boy. I didn't need her to get to Nashville and I didn't want her cheap brand of sex. But I would carry with me some of the lies she taught me about love. I had bought some of her propaganda and it had caused a shift within me. It was another type of power I was learning to use, only I could choose when and how to use it.

I still talked to Paul on the phone. I knew better than to believe everything Crystal had said and there was definitely a part of me that wondered if it was really true. Plus, I needed Paul. He was part of my future, my life in Nashville. I couldn't bring myself to ask him about it. If I could just believe that it never happened or if it did, that it wasn't his fault, I could keep him. I would fall asleep at night imagining I was successful in Nashville, that he and I were in love, and that everyone knew us as that awesome, adorable, tour-manager-or-whatever-couple. He fit perfectly into my life plan.

Paul came to visit me in Westville the next month, the day I took my SAT's. I was a nervous wreck. It was maybe not the best day for him to fly in as I found myself distracted by my excitement and I needed so badly to do well. According to the requirements for the Early Admission program, I had to get at least an 1110. That was the magic number: 1110. I did not want to be stuck in Westville for another year so I wished with every answer that I filled out with the No. 2 pencil for an 1110.

Paul was there by the time I got home from the test and it was nice to put my worries aside and relax with him. It snowed a lot, so we didn't leave the house much. Instead, we watched movies and played pool in the basement. We laughed a lot and flirted. He was very affectionate and I didn't mind at all. At night I would sneak down to the den, where he was staying on the sleeper sofa. We would kiss for a while before I would tiptoe back to my room, being careful to avoid the creaking top stair.

He didn't ask about Crystal at all. I mentioned casually that we hadn't been hanging out and his response was that she didn't seem like the kind of friend I needed. He really believed in me and like so many others, he saw her as trouble. That was all I needed to hear.

March, 2000.

I went to Nashville a second time for an interview at Belmont, another program requirement. I sat in a room with all kinds of fancy recording equipment that I had only seen before on TV, hoping I looked very collegiate in my navy sweater and a khaki skirt. I sat up straight, crossed my legs, and rested my hands in my lap. Determination and infatuation took me over and later I couldn't remember a single thing I said to the guy.

Afterwards, we took a formal tour of the school and the recording studio. The halls were lined with gold records: Reba McEntire, Tricia Yearwood, Vince Gill and so many others. I couldn't believe that this place existed somewhere outside my dreams, that these could be my halls and that this could be my life. I thought about the students there, the large number of people who loved music as much as I did, who wanted to make a life out of it and how I wanted so badly to be a part of such a community. At home, I was the only person I knew who was like that.

Paul took me to dinner and then to his house. My parents said I had to be back to the hotel by midnight. Paul and I put on a movie in his bedroom but we talked and kissed through the whole thing, my white halter-top coming off in a moment of passion. I lay on the bed in my jeans and bra, feeling exposed but not quite nervous about it. He lay next to me, propped up on one elbow as he ran his fingertips over my bare stomach.

I felt safe. I trusted Paul. I hoped this might blossom into a relationship. I had enjoyed daydreaming about it but I didn't feel any more invested than he seemed to be. I didn't want any more from him than he was willing or able to give. We enjoyed spending time together, we respected and admired each other and the rest would happen as it happened. I kissed him again and then turned away from him to put my shirt back on, laughing lightly; he drove me back to the hotel where my parents were waiting up for me.

One day in the spring, I got a letter in the mail that I knew was my SAT scores. I believed I was a smart girl but I didn't work as hard as I could have in school and I had been so nervous and distracted the day I took the test. I tore open the top of the envelope with my thumb. I unfolded the letter and my eyes flew over the page for the place where there was a number printed.

ONE - THREE THROWS FOR A DOLLAR

1110.

2

tick tock

I was in. I was leaving for Nashville in six months. I quit my after school job as a hostess at Applebee's and didn't participate in cheerleading or ballet for the rest of the year. This was my last semester of high school and I was going to enjoy it for all it was worth.

May, 2000.
One day, when I was driving my brother home from school, he told me that some guy in his class wanted him to tell me "hello." His name was Chase. I didn't know who he was but I was excited and surprised, even, that someone had noticed me. The next day Chase asked him to tell me "I love you" from him. I had to figure out who this guy was!

TWO - TICK TOCK

Later that week, my brother and I were leaving the school parking lot when he pointed and said, "Hey, that's Chase." I followed his finger to a guy wearing silver pants and a black long sleeved shirt. He had brown hair with blonde streaks in the front, which on him managed to look more punk rock than preppy. He was walking down the sidewalk with a friend, talking and laughing. As we drove by, he saw me and started fanning himself as if to say, "She's so hot." He didn't know I could see him.

I was certainly curious. He was cute, he was different and he was interested in me. I wanted so badly for someone to know that I was different, too. Maybe he could tell I didn't belong there.

A few days later, I dressed up for an after school field trip to Pittsburgh with the French Club. I was wearing a turquoise and black paisley silk skirt and a sheer black shirt over a blue tank top. I liked to think I was on the cutting edge of fashion without drawing too much attention to myself but that day I was feeling a little extra bold. I put blue food coloring streaks in my hair, and though blue on blonde looks more like green, I went with it anyway. When I got home that night my brother gave me a note, folded into a small square.

Kim,

Before I start, let me say the green is beautiful in your hair. I realize I know nothing about you, but I know I want to. And I know I don't know what makes you tick, but I plan on finding out.

I don't really know what to say. I mean, I guess it's up to you for what happens next.

555-0352 (ask for Chase)

"I wanna be the last thing that you hear when you're falling asleep."

I love the Counting Crows.

<3,

Chase

Of course I would call him. He wanted to be the last thing I heard when I was falling asleep! Who says that? To someone he's never even met! I was excited about the prospect of romance—real romance. With someone who quotes beautiful lyrics and wears silver pants and likes when I do something ridiculous like dye my hair green. Someone with whom I could be myself.

I called him the next day after school. I was beyond nervous, my heart pounding so loudly I was worried he would hear it over the phone.

TWO - TICK TOCK

"Is Chase there?" I asked the woman who answered. I waited for her to get him.

"Hello?"

"Hi. This is Kim."

"Well hello!"

"Hello." I smiled. This was going well.

I told him about the French Club trip. He told me about his guitar playing, the songs he was writing and how he hated school and found it completely pointless. I told him I missed doing theatre because I didn't have a show that spring. He said he had seen me in the school's production of *Poe's Midnight Dreary* the previous fall before he knew who I was. He had a friendly voice and an offbeat sense of humor. I sensed complicated emotions swirling beneath his casual words.

He invited me to a show he was playing at a small theatre in town. It would be the first time we met in person. I already had plans that night but I wouldn't have missed this for the world so I rushed over, on my own, as soon as I could. I was late and when I walked in, he was alone on the stage, sitting on a stool with an acoustic guitar in his lap. I was wearing my favorite shirt, a soft sea green knit, jeans and my silver fairy charm on a chain that I wore almost every day.

He announced to the dark crowded room that he would play just one more song. Someone made a disappointed sound, to which Chase replied, "Dry your eyes, kitten." Then he played a Black Lab song:

She walks through the gates of the country, hands at her side
And I smile as I watch her walk by
Somehow I see there are ships in her eyes
She's better off now

I was impressed with his voice, his song choice and his charm. I was smitten.

We went on our first date a few nights later. We walked down to the lake and sat on a weathered bench by the dock. He anxiously picked at the peeling white paint. I was also nervous but I hoped I was better at hiding it.

"So you grew up here, at the lake?" he asked.

"Yeah, I have like a hundred cousins and all my uncles have boats. We spent our summers on the lake, swimming or tubing or watching the fireworks at the park."

"That's so nice. You're lucky. Our family is... Well, I don't see anyone much except Mum and my brother. And my brother and I aren't very close."

He put his arm around me and I rested my head on his shoulder, feeling the sun on my face. I didn't know what to say back. "I'm sorry," or "that's awful," seemed so cliché, so I just looked up at him into his big blue eyes.

I'm sorry, I thought. *That's awful. But now you have me.*

Then he kissed me. Despite my nervousness, I felt very comfortable with him. It was as if it was a first kiss and a thousandth kiss at the same time.

Back at my house, we watched my favorite movie, *Playing By Heart*. We were both more at ease now. Our kiss had broken the ice and we were beginning to settle into each other's company. I didn't want the night to end. I wanted to look into his eyes, kiss him and be with him forever.

He nicknamed me Kitten and called me only that. We had so much to say to each other, like we'd been quiet our whole lives until we met. It was as if I had underestimated how hungry I was for a companion, how much I needed to be understood, to be pursued, to be seen and to be reflected in someone's eyes. And he fed that hunger with his words, both verbally and in the letters we exchanged between classes when we passed each other in the halls at school.

```
Kitten,
So, Spanish sucks. I'm never going to Spain,
so why am I learning this stuff, ya know? I'm
thinking about you. How I just can't seem to
```

get enough of you. I could drink a case of you and still be on my feet. I can't get you out of my head, and I think you shine when you smile. I haven't felt this way about someone in a long time. All I can say is I'm looking forward to being with you as long as I can. I'm pretending I'm a pirate and you're my treasure. Now, to enjoy the spoils of this find. Think about it. It makes sense. Seriously, it does.
"Can I keep you?"
Chase

He had a hunger too, which he let show without fear. He wasn't needy or whiny; rather, it came across more like he was in awe of me, felt lucky to have me and didn't believe he deserved me. It was nice to be so treasured but I didn't see it the way he did. I felt lucky to have him.

I told Paul about Chase, of course. I wasn't worried that he would be upset about it. I knew we were friends more than anything and that he wasn't trying to create a commitment out of our relationship. He was just as understanding as I thought he'd be, happy for me even. We still talked on the phone once or twice a week about what he was up to in his work, about my upcoming move to Nashville or my final months of high school life.

The girls and I had planned to go to Prom together, sans dates and I couldn't think of a better way to enjoy one of my last high school milestones than to be with my best friends. I wore a pale blue Cinderella gown that laced up the back and a tiara, which sparkled atop a pile of curls.

Chase joined me for the after party at Meredith's house. All the girls changed into pajamas and all the boys seemed anxious. Chase got along with everyone but we kept mostly to ourselves, setting up camp on the floor in the den. It was the first time I had spent the night next to a guy but that didn't occur to me. There was nothing outside of that room at that moment. We curled up together in my navy blue sleeping bag from the summer camp that I had outgrown and whispered late into the night. We had so much to learn about each other.

"There are some things I want to tell you, Kitten but I'm nervous because I don't want to scare you away. I already have no idea what you see in me. I have had a lot of turmoil in my life and the person that I am is the end result of everything I've done."

"You can tell me anything," I said. "I'm not going anywhere." I put my hand on his chest.

"I just, I wish there was a way for you to see inside me. I've never felt this way about anyone or anything. I'm happier right now in my life than I thought was humanly possible," he said, his tone serious.

He told me that his dad and his mom had split up when he was really young and that he had chosen not to speak to his dad anymore at an age too young for such a decision; he was now in the process of starting to cultivate a relationship with this man who was his father but who he hardly knew. He told me everything.

"I used to play sports," he continued. "I was actually really good. But in seventh grade...depression hit me really hard. It was hard for me to watch my friends change. In eighth grade, I lost a friend that was the only thing I still enjoyed in my life. We were inseparable for eight years then one day he...quit. The summer between eighth and ninth grade I barely left the house except to go to therapy, and when I hit rock bottom I tried to kill myself twice."

I brushed his hair from his eyes. He had just added red streaks to the front of it, where the blonde had been. He went on.

"Looking back I don't regret it but my life has never been the same. They put me on these pills to help me open up to people again. Then I didn't have the energy to kill myself so I just kept marching on in my one-man army. Then I

TWO - TICK TOCK

fell really hard for you. I was so happy that day. That was the day I found the gun. I remember being happier than I felt was possible and I didn't want to lose that feeling so I thought about ending my life again. But I couldn't do it. You were the reason I didn't. You saved my life."

I just shook my head and then I kissed him. Truly, none of that scared me. I was girly and friendly and my family life was happy but many days I felt like I was on the inside what Chase was on the outside. I always believed I was a happy person with a sad soul. I felt like I had had tragedy in my life when I hadn't. Somehow, without having experienced what he had, his scars resonated with me.

"You wanted to know my story, now you do. I hope I haven't scared you away," he said.

"You haven't. You couldn't. Nothing you do could keep me away," I reassured him.

We marveled at each other. I could see him. I knew who was behind those big blue eyes.

It was an incredible feeling to be so important to someone, to be treasured. I needed him for different reasons than he needed me but just as much. He helped me to see ways in which I could express myself artistically. He showed me not to be so afraid to be different or to be misunderstood. We each wanted to see the world how the other did.

From a very young age, I found myself to be completely preoccupied with love. Not fairy-tale love but passionate, devastating, haunting love. Now it seemed I had found someone who felt the same way.

One day in school, I saw Chase in the hall on my way to third period Algebra and he gave me a note that he had probably written in Spanish class. I slid into my seat next to Meredith and held up my calculator proudly. She had a sheet of gold star stickers in her textbook. Any day that I remembered to bring my calculator she gave me a gold star. "Yay, Ims!" she said, using her special nickname for me, before she passed me my brand new star. I added it to the three others on the cover of my notebook and we laughed.

As the teacher began to go over our homework, I opened the note. It was blank. I turned it over but still nothing. Then I saw it at the bottom of the page in very light pencil, a line from *Playing By Heart*: "Is it too late to say I love you?"

Finally I remembered to bring my calculator to class but then I forgot how to use it. The teacher was speaking in gibberish and everyone around me disappeared. I may as well have been lazing in the field at home, under a dancing willow tree and dreaming.

TWO - TICK TOCK

I was Faith Hill CDs, giggling with my girlfriends and reading books under a big sky. He was black fingernails, blue hair and Stone Temple Pilots, and I loved him.

But I was leaving in the fall. Soon! I had to be honest with him about that. We only had a matter of months to be together before I would be starting college six hundred miles away and he would have two years of high school to finish. I didn't know how we would make it work but we would have to find a way. Chase agreed that somehow we would survive.

```
Kitten,
May I say that you look absolutely beautiful
today? My jaw fell off and my heart just about
stopped beating when I saw you this morning. I
still can't believe you're mine. You don't
need to worry about losing me kitten; this is
real. I'm not going to let any distance be-
tween you and I affect love. We fit perfectly,
ya know? No, really, we do. I love you, and
not just in that nighttime television sort of
way. Kitten, you are my hourglass. I could
watch you for eternity. Just give me that
chance.
Zoro
```

I didn't let myself think about being afraid of what would happen. I just couldn't put the two thoughts—Chase and college—together in my mind.

We spent that summer in his bed, which isn't at all how it sounds. We would just lie there and watch movies or talk for hours. We talked about his concern for his mom's happiness, about music, about movies, about my need to get out of Westville and do something bigger, about his struggles with self-confidence and about the intense passion we felt for each other. We were both Scorpios so the entire relationship was very intense. We weren't just testing the waters. We were swimming in an ocean.

The passion was more physical than I'd had before and while we talked a lot about sex, Chase didn't pressure me to go farther than I wanted to. I'm not saying we were angels but I drew the line and we left it there.

One particularly overcast and humid day we were in his room deciding on a movie.

"*Muppets Christmas* or *Muppets Take Manhattan*?" he asked. I was quiet for a minute, watching him ponder over the videos stacked on the TV before snuggling further under the brown blanket. It was cold without him next to me.

"Or we could always watch..."

TWO - TICK TOCK

"*Return to Oz!*" I finished.

"Ok, Ozma, that it is."

Chase was the first person I'd ever met who agreed with me that *Return to Oz* was amazing and not a bit creepy. He called me Ozma and I called him Tick Tock after two characters in the movie.

He pushed play and crawled over me to his spot on the bed. He put his arms around me and turned me towards him. I didn't really need to see the movie anyway. I'd seen it five hundred times.

"You saved me, you know. I never thought I'd feel like this about anyone. I love you, Kit," he said.

His gigantic blue eyes burned into mine and I knew he meant it. It was scary and exhilarating. I wanted nothing more than to stay in that moment forever, swimming in his eyes and covered in his hands.

"I love you, too," I said and he kissed me.

"Look, Billina," said Dorothy on the TV, "these ones have lost their heads."

3 ships in her eyes

August, 2000.

We had lost our heads. We had also lost all sense of time and reality and an eagerness to imagine the future. I saw Chase. That was all. I saw him and I saw us and nothing else mattered. When I spoke of Nashville or of my excitement for college, it felt like I was speaking of someone else's life. Not my own. Not mine with him.

But the truth was that I did have to leave. I was older than he was and it was my time to go out on my own. The truth was that it didn't matter that I loved him. I could hope he would follow, that we would find our way to each other but I was leaving and my life was about to be very, very different.

THREE – SHIPS IN HER EYES

A week before I was to leave for Nashville, Dad and I began packing everything I could take into the back of his red Ford truck. When Chase got off work that afternoon I drove over to his house and we sat down on the couch. It felt strange to be on the couch because we were so often in the sanctuary of his bedroom. Saffron, one of Chase's mom's birds sat on my knee.

I could hardly get the words out.

"I don't want it to be like this," I said, my hands clasped in my lap. If I squeezed my hands together hard enough, I thought, maybe I could keep from crying.

"Saffron," said Saffron.

"But there is so much that I need to experience at school. I love you and I don't want to stop talking or say it's over forever, but I need to be on my own right now."

"Saffron."

"Yes, you too, Saffron," said Chase to the bird, trying to show strength in his shaky voice.

"And you have two years of school left before we could even be in the same place," I said, "and I don't know if you would ever want to live in Nashville."

Chase was crying, which really upset me. I needed to stop talking. I was quiet for a minute. I reached for him and we held each other.

Finally he pulled away and looked in my eyes.

"I understand," he said. "I knew this was coming but that doesn't make it any easier."

What else could we have done? I would rather have ended it on a high note and have been able to come back to him later than try to make it work, disastrously, and do irreparable damage to something so amazing. I told him what time we were leaving for Nashville and it was up to him whether or not he wanted to come see me off. Then I left.

I cried on the drive home, warm tears leaving spots on the front of my blue tank top. I hoped he would come to see me before I left. I didn't want him to be angry. To feel sad that we were broken up was inevitable for both of us but nothing would be worse than if this kept us from a future we were meant to have. I wondered if he would show up to see me off, if this was really the end or just the end for now, if we could still love each other even if we weren't together.

Saying goodbye to my friends was much more pleasant. Meredith and some of the other girls met me out for ice cream. We all shared the *Dream Boat*, which is a giant bowl filled with 24 scoops of various kinds of ice cream and every topping imaginable. We dug in with long silver spoons and ate until we were silly from the sugar. Then we stuck in straws and drank the melted ice-cream puddle left at the bottom of the huge bowl until we were sick.

THREE – SHIPS IN HER EYES

One of the girls started choking. "I sucked up a nut," she said once she regained her breath and we laughed until we cried. Those tears felt good to cry.

The following morning my parents and I left for Nashville and the girls came to see me off. I stood chatting with them in the driveway, the early morning fog beginning to rise from the fields. We were talking about the girls coming to visit me in Nashville when Meredith changed the subject.

"Is Chase coming?" she asked softly.

"I'm not sure. I left it up to him. I hope he does but if not I..."

Just then I saw his mom's car turn in to the driveway down by the barns. I smiled sadly, relieved he had come but dreading yet another goodbye.

I thought of a quote from one of Chase's letters. *I will go anywhere she goes. Chauffeur the bags of a precious lover. I will go anywhere she goes. Sleep on the pillow that reeks of another.*

I turned back to Meredith. "Yes. Yes, he's coming," I said, flashing Meredith a smile that I knew she could read as happy-in-the-moment but not happy-in-my-heart. I knew she was the kind of friend who would be there for me when I needed her, then or ever, like the promise we had made to each other: *super glue.*

Everything else went by in a blur and I found myself in the back seat of the truck on the road in Ohio. I flipped through my high school yearbook. Meredith wrote a whole page on how proud of me she was and how she was my biggest fan. Jeff Meyers claimed a page toward the back. He wrote, "Have fun in Nashville," with his address and a sketch of a sun with a face. I traced the flames with my fingers. Goodbye.

I slept for a while, lulled to sleep by Dramamine and exhaustion from the morning's tears and the urge to dream of what this day would bring. Once I was awake again, somewhere in Kentucky, I asked mom to put my Dixie Chicks CD in the stereo and I sang along softly.

There's no mercy in a live wire. No rest at all in freedom. The choices we are given, it's no choice at all. The proof is in the fire you touch before it moves away. You must always know how long to stay and when to go.

The words resonated with me. As hard as it was to leave Chase, I knew it was my time to leave. I knew how long to stay and when to go.

THREE – SHIPS IN HER EYES

Finally, we reached Nashville. The skyline appeared in the distance, a sight that was becoming familiar to me. We ate dinner and stayed in a hotel. *Tomorrow*, I thought, crawling into my hotel bed. Tomorrow I wouldn't have time for nostalgia. Tomorrow my heart would be full of anticipation. Tomorrow I would be Kim Carlson, Belmont student and resident of Nashville, Tennessee, with my whole life in front of me. *Tomorrow I will put Westville behind me and step into my new life.*

In the morning, we pulled up in front of Wright Hall, the brick U-shaped girl's dormitory. Parents and new students were unloading cars with license plates from everywhere: Texas, Oregon, Maryland. I had never met anyone from Texas, Oregon or Maryland. My world was growing exponentially larger and not a moment too soon.

We took the elevator to the fourth floor and checked in with my Resident Assistant, Anna. She was the smallest and peppiest person I had ever met.

"Welcome to Belmont," she said, making an effort to really pronounce the "t" at the end and clasping her hands in front of her like one of the Von Trapp children. "Where are you from?" she asked us.

"Pennsylvania!" my mom said, adjusting her tone to mirror Anna's. My parents talked with Anna while I watched my new neighbors coming and going from the elevator, boxes in hand.

Mom made a point of telling Anna that I was only 17 and really just a senior in high school. Anna looked at me quizzically, trying to figure out if I might need consolation when my parents left. If she only knew I had begged to be sent to boarding school at the age of ten. I loved my parents but I was ready for this.

Anna showed me her room, the first one on the right and then mine, number 417.

"Let me know if you need anything," she said. "I'll be just" - sharp t - "down the hall." She smiled at my parents and tucked a strand of stick-straight blonde hair behind her ear. "I'll see you guys later!"

We spent the rest of the morning unloading the truck and the afternoon trying to figure out where to put everything. I met my roommate and her family. She was tall with straw colored hair cropped neatly below her chin, dressed casually in jeans, a T-shirt and tennis shoes. She was friendly but quiet. She didn't really make eye contact with me when we chatted; rather, she just looked around the room or into boxes. I thought maybe she didn't know what to think of me.

When her parents were ready to leave, we all stood in a circle holding hands and prayed. I knew that my parents

THREE – SHIPS IN HER EYES

were relieved that her family prayed together too. A few months earlier, mom had ordered a book for me called, *How to Stay Christian in College*. I would never open it. It was like when I was in the seventh grade and she brought home from the library a book about periods, trying to prepare me for something I was just going to have to experience firsthand. Each ended up stashed under my bed. I didn't question my faith; I just didn't want to read about it in a book like that. I wondered if my roommate was the same way.

Then, my parents and I had the dorm room to ourselves and they sat on either side of me on the bed, one of the few pieces of furniture in my tiny new room. Mom pulled a small present out of her purse. It was a children's book called, *The Kissing Hand*, about a little raccoon who goes off to school. His Mom kisses the palms of his hands each morning so he has her with him all day long and so he won't be scared at school. Then Mom kissed the center of my left palm and Dad, my right. We stood there and hugged.

When they left I could feel their sadness. Dad had tears in his eyes, which was unsettling to me. I had only occasionally seen him cry and there was something strange about seeing my father that way. This time, it was my fault. I went over to my window and watched through the blinds. I saw them walk to the truck. Dad opened the door for Mom.

They waved and though I wasn't sure they could really see me, I waved too.

I felt torn between paralyzing fear and an overwhelming excitement. Turning to my quiet dorm room, I thought, *This is my home now. No matter what happens, there's no going back.*

September, 2000.

I loved walking to class. The campus was beautiful, covered in flowered trellises, intricate gazebos and elegant statues. There were new people everywhere, playing guitars in the grass and walking in all directions. I loved the freedom of my days; it was all so different from high school. I had an early morning tennis class and then a break until eleven o'clock when I would go to Artist Management class and then to Sociology after grabbing a pack of pop-tarts from the corner market. Other days I could sleep later before I had Marketing and Statistics classes.

I met some people in my classes but no one asked me to hang out. My friendliness was often shrouded by my reluctance to chat with strangers. I never regretted missing my senior year but I was surprised at how lonely I could feel while surrounded by all these people who were just like me.

THREE – SHIPS IN HER EYES

I expected to feel more at home than ever and instead I found myself yearning for close friends.

Chase and I chatted sometimes. We tried not to talk often since technically we were broken up but we missed each other and I didn't have a lot of other company. My roommate, who was older and should have been more ready for college than I was homesick for her nearby hometown in Kentucky, yet somehow she seemed to be making friends and fitting in easily. This perplexed and frustrated me. Was I destined to be as invisible here as I had been in high school?

One afternoon I was alone in the dorm room after class. Through the window, the sky was bright blue, the kind of fall day that I should have been enjoying outside with friends. But I had no one to call and there was no one to invite me to join in their trip to a park or whatever the other students were doing. I didn't even know yet what there was to do. So I sat at my desk, an open textbook shoved off to the side and a deserted chat window open on my computer. A Faith Hill song played on the stereo: *It just isn't right. I've been two thousand miles down a dead-end road. Let me let go.*

Chase had just signed offline after giving me some short answers about how life was "sucky." He wasn't being responsive to me and wasn't letting me have access to him. The distance between us was greater than the six hundred miles that separated us. I didn't know how to fix it.

I felt overwhelmed by emotions that were unfamiliar to me. Fear, loneliness, uncertainty, all of this broke open inside me and I didn't know how to release it. Tears didn't seem big enough. Words, well, there was no one to talk to. Determined now to find some way, any way, I took a small X-Acto knife out of my desk drawer. I had used it on some school project. I pulled the leg of my sweatpants up to my thigh. There were ancient first bike-ride scars on my knee so if the cut left a mark it wouldn't seem suspicious or out of place. I gripped the orange plastic that surrounded the blade and drew a small line no longer than half an inch across my knee with the sharp metal tip, and I watched as the point left a scarlet trail in its wake.

Suddenly, I felt calm. I took a breath that felt like the first breath I had ever taken in the world. I had just been born again. Suddenly, I knew I would make friends and everything would be fine with Chase. Whatever had seemed so pressing on my mind wasn't so pressing anymore.

I hobbled slowly across the room, not that I needed to hobble because it didn't really hurt, and I pressed the cut with a piece of tissue paper until the bleeding stopped. It wasn't blood I was after; it was peace.

I finally made friends with Megan, a girl who lived down the hall. She and her roommate were welcoming to me

THREE – SHIPS IN HER EYES

when I was bored and wanted to hang out in their room and they invited me to come along when they went to Target or out to dinner. I didn't feel like a burden to them. Megan, who was from "North Carolahnah," as it sounded in her heavy accent also loved country music more than life itself and was a music business major. She was shorter than me with curly blonde hair and a big smile, indicative of her big personality.

Classes, bad cafeteria food and group study sessions, life was turning into a pretty typical freshman year at college, except when I would walk down the hall of my dorm and I would hear one girl singing and playing the keyboard and another practicing her fiddle. Walking across campus, there would be a guy strumming his acoustic guitar in a gazebo and a group of students jamming around the grand piano in Neely Hall. I loved that music was everywhere. When I felt like a kite tumbling scared on the wind, music was my string—my connection to the ground.

I still held on to Chase like there was a string tied between us too. I couldn't let him go and I guess he couldn't let me go either. Even if he was trying to shut me out, the letters still came and though they were always welcome, each one left me feeling confused. Should I be happy he wrote or sad that we were apart and that this was continuing to hurt him?

Hurting both of us.

He wrote about wearing a cape to school or dying his hair purple, he wrote that he still loved me, more than ever and that he still loved me even if I was happier with other people in my life. But I wasn't. It was harder than I thought to be away from him. I liked college and I loved Nashville but I lit up inside every time I got a letter from him. It was clear for both of us the passion was just as strong but he had two years of high school to go so we still knew we couldn't be together now. We were stuck.

Chase was as torn as I was. As the weather grew colder so did his letters. *Companionship is hard to convey with someone you see once every few months,* he wrote. We fought because he didn't know anything about my new life and didn't seem to want to be a part of it but when he offered to visit I would turn him down. I was afraid to let him see my new life for fear that he might reject it. I wanted to continue to hope he would love it here like I did and to dream that eventually he would come to stay. Once he saw Nashville, I wouldn't be able to just hope any longer. I would know how he felt about it and that terrified me. Finally, tired after two months of arguing about it, I agreed to let him visit.

The plane tickets were a gift from his mother for his October 30th birthday. He appeared in the airport terminal wearing a leather jacket and a cowboy hat. *That's not him.*

THREE – SHIPS IN HER EYES

What is he trying to pull off? I want him just the way he is, I thought. Seeing him dressed so differently made my unease more palpable but he was trying to show his openness to Nashville and I recognized that.

Autumn was in full swing, brilliant red leaves on trees lining the sidewalks to my dorm, golden yellow as the sun by the historic mansion that was the visual highlight of the school. I walked with Chase all over the campus. *This is my world. Isn't it beautiful? Don't you want to be a part of this?* I showed him around school and introduced him to people I knew. Most of them had heard about him because you couldn't know me without knowing about Chase.

He wasn't allowed to stay overnight in the dorm with me because Belmont is a Christian school and they had strict rules about visitation in the dorms. My roommate and her new boyfriend agreed to rent a hotel room with us so we could all get off campus for the weekend. It felt very grown up. I wished we could have had our own hotel room but that seemed unfathomable, far off from where we were in our lives and in our relationship.

Chase and I had talked before about when or if we would have sex. I wanted to wait and though he made it clear that that was one of the many ways he wanted to show me he loved me, he supported my decision and didn't ever complain. This was the first time since prom night we had spent the night together. If it hadn't been for my roommate and her boyfriend in the room near us or my fear, I may not have been able to keep my promise to myself. But I did.

On Saturday we went to the mall. I hadn't been in Nashville long enough to know how to show someone the town and though neither of us really cared to be in the mall, it was something to do. After we were bored of wandering around the stores, we walked across the parking lot to where the riverboat docks and sat on the ground under a wooden gazebo. The sky was overcast and Chase was smoking a cigarette, which I held for him between drags. I loved holding his cigarettes.

"You seem really happy, Kit."

"Yeah, I guess. This is kind of where I belong, I think."

"Right, I can see it."

"You would like it here too," I told him. "There's so much music and not just country. There is a lot of rock too. So many of the kids at Belmont, I've been to their shows and you would love this stuff."

"I can't afford to come here. I am going to have to stay close to home for school, Kit, or move somewhere and not go to school just, like, get a job."

"We can make it work," I assured him.

"I want to but I don't see how," he said, defeated.

THREE – SHIPS IN HER EYES

He stubbed out his cigarette butt. My hands felt empty when he didn't hand it back to me. I reached out and held his hand. We were quiet for a few minutes.

"I'm not saying no or anything," he said finally. "I just don't know yet what I want. I do love you. That's all I can say right now."

"I understand," I said.

"You're cold. Let's get back."

I tucked the Camel coupon from his cigarette pack into my pocket, a souvenir of the moment where he said *maybe*. I would hold on to his maybe for as long as it would take, even forever.

November, 2000.

I went home for a long weekend to take care of some things regarding my pending graduation and to see my friends. It was weird walking down the high school's hallways again. I remembered emptying out my locker just a few months before with Chase standing next to me, watching me prepare to leave him. Even though I always came back, he said he was always watching me leave.

On the video we made documenting my last day of school, Chase was holding the camera while I put notebooks and scraps of paper into my backpack.

"I'm picking your nose," he said, his finger positioned to create that illusion on the video.

"Okay," I laughed, un-sticking pictures from the inside of my locker door and putting them into my backpack: a new one of Chase and me, one of the Dixie Chicks, one of me with Meredith and the girls.

"Now I'm staring at your ass," he said, positioning the camera on my white shorts.

"Umm, Ok," I said, smiling at him, a glimmer in my eyes.

Chase appeared in front of me then. It was between classes and the halls were filled with students talking noisily and slamming lockers. He was holding a white carnation in his hand. He handed me the flower and bowed a little and he kissed me. I could feel the other students' eyes on us. Did they know what a special moment this was? That I wasn't just another student kissing her boyfriend in the hall? Looking closer, I realized he had written, "I love you" on every petal on the flower. He also handed me a letter, which I read in the car before I left the school parking lot.

```
Kitten,
Welcome home, baby.  I don't really know what
to say.  I've missed you so fuckin' much.  It's
not even something I can describe with a pen
```

THREE – SHIPS IN HER EYES

and paper. I love you. I guess I always have, and I know I always will. I'm sorry for what we've been through in the past few months, but this is new for both of us, right? We're an army. We're a tank. We can't be stopped, and I won't take that chance.

I didn't know how we could be together or if we could make it work. But there was one thing I was sure of—there was no one like Chase in all the world.

We saw each other again when I came home for Christmas. He gave me a gray garden statue of an angel with the word "Faith" engraved at her feet. He said he walked by her and thought, "Kit has to have that!" I loved her. She was sad and romantic and hopeful just like me. There were a lot of things I cared about that Chase didn't—Jesus, country music, clothes—but he loved me for exactly who I was. He still saw me even as I changed. He still chose me. He also gave me the infinity ring he always wore on his pinky finger, the ring he hardly ever took off. I wore it on my left hand.

I knew what he wanted from me. I told him I was ready and we set a date for a couple of nights before I was set to leave for Nashville again. At home and getting ready, I was so scared I thought I might be sick. We had fooled around plenty over the last year but I was nervous anyway. I wanted everything to be perfect. I put on a black shirt, a tan suede skirt and black heels and set off for his house.

When I got there, he had a hundred candles lit in his room and he was at least as nervous as I was, if not more. I took off my shoes and lay down on the bed. He followed, wrapped his arms around me and brought his face near to mine.

"I love you, Kit. I always have and I always will."

"I love you, too," I whispered.

My heart was beating so fast I thought it would explode. He kissed me and began to take my clothes off. I wondered how this moment compared to all of the times I'd imagined it in the past.

I still had no idea how we were going to make it work but I was certain that somehow we would be together. I felt sure and secure and was suddenly devoid of all my anxieties. I had found the peace I'd been grappling for.

Or so I thought.

January, 2001.

I had cut my knee a few times that first semester before Chase and I had things moderately settled, which had in turn settled me; however, upon returning to school from the

THREE – SHIPS IN HER EYES

holidays, I found the unease crawling back into me and I searched for another way to feel relief from the stress of feeling out of control of my life.

Megan and I made friends with a girl who was in her sorority and who was in my recording technology class. Brittany was a year older than us and seemed to me to be extremely self-assured. She was always laughing at someone or something. She wore giant fake blonde ponytails and tons of mascara. She was taller than us and wore tight jeans and preppy sweaters over her curves. One night she invited us over to her Belmont apartment to hang out with her roommate and some guys.

It was much harder for Belmont to enforce their rules at the apartments. There were no cameras or a front desk. When we got there they had all been drinking and were talking very loudly. Once they caught on that Megan and I had never had a drink before, they decided it was their calling to show us how it was done. Brittany's boyfriend poured me a shot of Jack Daniels and popped open a can of Diet Coke.

"Okay, the Diet Coke is your chaser," he explained. "Have a little sip first then down the shot as fast as you can. Don't even let it hit your mouth, just straight down your throat. Then drink more Coke to get the taste out."

Oh my gosh. This is going to be awful. But...well, why not?

61

I couldn't think of one good reason not to do it so I braced myself and then drank the shot, finding it hard not to taste the strong liquor. The flavor lingered and my throat burned. I coughed a little but quickly drank from the Coke can again.

Not bad at all, I thought.

Everything changed.

March, 2001.

My college friends and I were still too young to take a worthwhile spring break trip so most of us went home. My parents were out of town, which suited me perfectly. One night Chase stayed over but the next night he had plans and I wanted to see the girls. Meredith brought some girlfriends with her from high school who came along with liquor and jello shots. Then the guys showed up with beer. We all got tanked and someone threw up in my parents' bathtub. A lot had changed in the seven or eight months I'd been gone.

I cleaned the house as best I could the next day. My parents still trusted me and I was letting them down; at least they didn't have to know about it.

Aside from our less-than-upstanding extracurricular activities, Megan and I joined a group for Music Business ma-

THREE – SHIPS IN HER EYES

jors called Service Corps, where members got to volunteer at various entertainment industry events. In February, we worked the Country Radio Seminar at the Convention Center. Radio DJs and programmers came in from all over the country to keep up on happenings in the radio industry and interview the stars. I personally escorted a gravelly-voiced country star at a press event, guiding him between radio station tables for his interviews and letting the DJs know when his time with them was up. It felt like a dream. Even if it was just for the day, I was handling the media opportunities for someone who used to seem larger than life. It suddenly felt like ages ago rather than just a few months ago that I would call the local Westville radio station and chat up the DJs about the latest music they were playing or what their jobs were like. My world was upside-down.

    At the Disco Party at the end of the weeklong seminar, I met several of the singers whose CDs were in my collection. I surprised myself by working up the nerve to ask Kenny Chesney to dance. "Maybe later!" he said, a gracious way of saying no. I didn't care; just being able to ask was all I wanted.

    Service Corps felt like the continued education to the studying and networking I'd begun at home, when I would memorize liner notes and find a way backstage at concerts.

Classes were important but in this industry, the connections and inside view of these events were the most beneficial.

A small edge I had over the other students was that I already had friends in the music industry: Paul, the band of brothers and a guy I'd met at a Dixie Chicks concert in Buffalo who had since become a country music television host. Of these, I saw Paul the most. He would pick me up at the dorm and take me to dinner or to shows. Then, we'd sit at Café Coco and talk about what I was learning and what he'd been working on lately. Even though I had once imagined that when I moved to Nashville we would be together, we were just good friends and that's all I wanted from him. We were in different phases of our lives but also my heart had changed since I'd met Chase.

As I neared the end of my freshman year, I felt that I had begun to accomplish what I'd set out to do. I was growing up, preparing for a career that excited me and I'd made friends. Chase and I, though we hadn't made any kind of exclusive commitment to each other, had survived a year apart.

One day that spring, Megan and I were hanging out, talking about life, boys and dreams. It was raining and there was nowhere to go, anyway. She told me she remembered meeting Chase when he had come to visit.

THREE – SHIPS IN HER EYES

"You were lying on the top bunk in your room," she said. "I remember he was playing with your hair, holding on to you like you were so fragile, like you were about to break."

"I don't remember that at all," I replied, thinking back to that last fall.

I liked the picture she painted. In that memory, Megan had captured a truth about us—I would break without him.

World War Three

May, 2001.

Even with Chase at home, I couldn't stand the thought of being in Westville all summer so I decided that taking some extra classes would be a more productive use of my time. I did have a month off and that was long enough for me. I was home just in time for prom and graduation. Megan went to spend the summer at home in North Carolina. Anna, my perky resident assistant, went home to Los Angeles. My roommate who had surprised us all by getting pregnant over Spring Break moved back to Kentucky. Megan and I would be rooming together in the apartments. I would move in when I got back to school in July and she would join me that fall.

FOUR – WORLD WAR THREE

My month at home was broken up by a trip to L.A. to visit Anna. She took me to see Rodeo Drive and Hollywood Boulevard, where she took a picture of me with my hands in Marilyn Monroe's handprints. I was fascinated by the city. When Anna was working, I would sit under a big tree in her family's yard and read my Bible. I had thrown myself into deep personal Bible study; I was reading scriptures, learning how to apply the verses to my life and writing vigorously about it in my journal.

When I was home again, I told Chase all about my newfound religious convictions and he wasn't totally supportive.

"Kit, I think it's attractive that you have something to believe in but it's just not for me," he said.

That was fine with me. We spent every day together until I left for Nashville again, though we kept arguing about my suddenly strengthened dedication to God's plan for my life. Finally we just decided it was something we couldn't talk about. Chase was Catholic but he wasn't sure what he believed in, and, really, he didn't have any kind of interest in thinking about it too much.

The thing we fought most about wasn't God or religion, it was that with my faith strengthened I did not want to have sex with him or even fool around as much as we had before. He felt rejected and he didn't understand why this was so important to me. It was hard for me to explain to someone who didn't have the upbringing that I had had or the beliefs I was trying to hold on to. Once we quit talking about it, things felt almost but not quite like the summer before. We stopped fighting but the rift was still there.

July, 2001.

Back in Nashville, I moved into my first real apartment. I brought my own furniture from home, the navy and black futon from my bedroom and the old brown couch from our basement. I loved having rooms to walk through, including a bathroom that would be just for us and my own bedroom; it was independence!

There was a guy who sat next to me in Music Publishing class and sometimes, we would make small talk together before class started or after it had ended. If he wasn't there one day, I would catch him up on what he missed and he would do the same for me. His name was Brian and he was from Atlanta. He was a year ahead of me and had transferred to Belmont that spring. He had dark spiky hair and he was tall, though he hunched a little. Most days he wore button-down shirts with loud floral prints or solid bright colors paired with khaki cargo shorts and sandals.

FOUR – WORLD WAR THREE

One day, in the elevator after class, Brian asked me if I would like to go to a show with him. It never hurts to make a new friend, I thought, especially since none of my friends were there for the summer, so I said yes. He took me to dinner and to see a country band play. He wore a black collared button-down shirt and his signature shorts and sandals. He asked tons of questions and seemed genuinely interested in the answers. He was polite and easy to talk to. I was surprised to find that I had a really nice time.

We went out again a few nights later. He would always pick me up even though our apartments were no more than a four-minute walk from each other. He would always come to my apartment door and open the door of his shiny red car for me. *A true southern gentleman,* I thought, *clearly raised well by his mother.*

At first, I didn't mention Brian to Chase or Chase to Brian. I felt there was no reason to throw it in Brian's face or to hurt Chase, and I was scared to discourage either of them. I just needed to see how this would play out.

I should have seen it coming. I had been out with Brian several times and I could tell he liked me but at that point, I still felt that I was just enjoying his company. One evening, after we had been out to dinner, I was sitting in an overstuffed chair in his apartment with my feet tucked underneath my legs.

"I'm gonna grab a beer. Would you like a drink?" he asked, getting up from the couch. His dark hair glistened in the dim evening light that seeped through the window, and he flashed me a smile that reached his eyes.

"Sure!" I said, smiling back. He knew my drink by then so I didn't have to specify.

When he came back, he handed me a cool glass of jack and coke, leaned over and kissed me. Just like that, I was surprised but I was more amazed by how good the kiss was; it was soft, sweet and confident. There were definitely sparks between us. At that moment, I began to think that maybe he was more than just someone to hang out with.

We continued to date through the summer. I began to find him truly charming: his chuckle, his ease in groups of people—something I'd always found difficult—as well as his generally happy mood. He was intelligent, he was a good listener, and most importantly he was encouraging. He thought I was fun and interesting and mature. He was also a little rebellious, which thrilled me. He came off as a wholly responsible, good guy but he wasn't a "goody-two shoes" and that suited me well.

I couldn't bring myself to tell Chase that I was seeing someone in Nashville. It was starting to seem inevitable that

FOUR – WORLD WAR THREE

he would have to know but I wasn't ready to cut ties there just yet. At some point, I found a way to work into a conversation with Brian that I had been dating someone back home, though not exclusively. He was really understanding about it. I guess he just figured, *Well I'm here and that guy's not*, and he was right. He was there every day to kiss me and talk to me and be an active part of my life. When it came time to make a decision, I chose to commit to Brian. It really came down to the fact that he was there and Chase wasn't and that wasn't Chase's fault.

When Megan moved in, we bought heavy black curtains to hang on the windows, painted the coffee table black before putting our handprints on it in blue. We covered the ugly brown sofa with a blue couch cover. I decorated my bedroom in pink and Megan decorated hers in purple. We made the apartment our home and it felt good.

Megan liked Brian. They would tease each other like brother and sister and the three of us started hanging out a lot. Brian would make us little pancakes with chocolate syrup, Megan would pick the movies and I would make the drinks. This was becoming routine.

We were in the living room one day with Brian and I on the couch and Megan on the futon, watching country music videos on CMT. It was early afternoon but no light came in to our black and blue room. *This is my life,* I thought. *I am here and Megan is my best friend and Brian is my, well, boyfriend. I can't deny it anymore.* Sitting there in the dark I knew, I couldn't keep Chase in the dark any longer. I went into my pink bedroom and lay on the bed in silence, staring at the twinkle lights above me. *Like fireflies in my own enchanted forest. If only I could believe in enchantment.*

In September, Megan rode the ten hours home with me to Westville for a weekend. She stayed with my family one evening while I went to Chase's house to tell him in person. We sat on the edge of his bed, each looking down at our knees. I was as kind as I could be. He wasn't as understanding this time. He didn't blame me, necessarily, though he was hurt and I was the cause of it. I showed my sadness but I was strong. This was my decision and the least I could do was to stand by it.

He wasn't shocked, I don't think. I knew the year I'd been gone had been hard for him too. He said he didn't want to talk to me for a while, and as hard as it would be for me to not be able to talk to him, I knew I had to respect his decision. We both needed time to heal. He wished me the best but I couldn't say the same words to him. It sounded like goodbye and I didn't want to say goodbye. It wasn't that I didn't love him, rather, it was that he was so far away and I

FOUR – WORLD WAR THREE

had no way of knowing if or when he would be able to follow me to Nashville. That had worn on me and having Brian in my life reminded me how great it was to be able to see someone every day. If Chase had been in Nashville I would have been with him, but that wasn't possible right now.

I drove back to the house where Megan was waiting for me and we lay on the sleeper sofa in the den until I was so tired from sobbing that I passed out. It was the worst pain I'd ever felt. My first heartbreak was a pinprick next to this cannonball hole. My heart was caving in, but I didn't see any other way. As much as I loved Chase, this was not something that we could hold on to. I had to grow up; it was time to build my new life.

Back at Belmont, Megan, Brian, and I were inseparable. Megan and I were enjoying a new level of independence in the apartments, where rules were nearly impossible for the school to enforce. Brian would buy us alcohol and we would all hang out in our apartment and drink or we would go over to Brittany's, whose apartment building was right across from ours. Sometimes we went out to Belmont parties, where they would have free drinks or dollar shots.

I didn't contact Chase as he had requested. I avoided being alone because that was when I would start thinking about him and wish to heaven I could hear his voice. I was distracted enough by Brian and Megan every waking moment. I was rarely without Brian every sleeping moment even though my bedroom only had a twin bed. He would often come over after I had already gone to sleep. He was with the guys, he always told me, but he never said where or what they were doing. He tasted of beer on those nights, and though I never drank beer, I loved the taste of it on his mouth.

I turned nineteen in November. All of our friends came over to our apartment, and Megan and I did a great job hosting, making sure no one was without a drink, especially ourselves. Earlier that day, Brian had given me a sapphire necklace that matched a ring he had given me the month before. I didn't know how to wear real jewelry like that but the gesture wasn't lost on me.

"Happy birthday, baby," he said, fastening the sparkling necklace over my Belmont t-shirt. He was practically bouncing with excitement.

"It's beautiful! I love this color," I said, touching the stone and admiring the deep blue. As I turned from the mirror it crossed my mind that I looked like a little girl playing dress up.

The rest of the semester went on very much the same way: in a haze of drinking, skipping a lot of class, forgetting

FOUR – WORLD WAR THREE

what was important to me. I became one-dimensional. My identity was made up completely by the presence of Megan on my right and Brian on my left. What music I liked, how I spent my time, and how I saw myself were defined by the two of them. I was as dependent on my little crew of two as they were on me.

Brian and I started talking about marriage and we agreed that we would wait until we were out of school, but we were in love and it was so fun to talk about who would be in the wedding. Megan would be maid of honor, of course, and the bridesmaids would wear pink. It would be in a beautiful coastal park in Georgia. We even picked out rings at the jewelry store where he had been shopping for me lately.

Despite the partying, we had all been raised in Christian families and had some semblance of a relationship with God. I had such a strong awareness of the importance of having God in my life that once I was on my own, the time when many people lose the drive to attend church, I had been visiting Nashville churches trying to find one that suited me. Though I was raised Catholic, I had chosen not to be confirmed and instead was considering other denominations. I felt that Catholicism had some wonderful traditions but was too based on God's laws and I thought that the teachings often overlooked the importance of God's love.

One Sunday, Megan and I visited a church that we had heard many Belmont students attended. It was called *River* and it was in the Brentwood area just south of Nashville. River was very evangelical. The leaders laid hands on people, the congregation was prone to throwing their hands in the air during songs or during the Sermon, and both the leaders and the church body spoke in tongues.

If I was looking for more passion in a Church, this one definitely had it. The pastor was very charismatic, with a blinding smile and humor in his Sermons. The music was fantastic, which is probably a big reason why Belmont students enjoyed the Church. Megan and I continued to attend and Brian often joined us. Sometimes, on our way to church, we would divert our path to the Cracker Barrel for breakfast instead but most weeks we at least tried to go.

I went home for Christmas break. Chase and I had hardly been in contact, but he knew I was in town and he wanted to see me. I wanted nothing more than to believe that there was still something there between us, even if now wasn't the time, and even if I was getting serious with Brian. It was as if there were two of me, Chase's Kit and Brian's Kim, and though only one was dominant at any given time, they both existed inside me, hoping and loving and aching.

FOUR – WORLD WAR THREE

Chase had rearranged his bedroom furniture. It felt strange to me, like there was less of me in it, like the memories we created together had been displaced. We put a movie on but mostly we just talked; we curled up on the bed with him sitting a safe distance away. He was completely closed off. I talked to fill the space, telling him about school and about some song lyrics I had been writing. I didn't know why, exactly, but I was still trying to show him how perfect we were for each other. Maybe I wanted him to fight for me or to wait for me. I made an effort not to talk about Brian and he didn't ask. I wanted so badly for him to touch me, to move closer to me and put his hand on my hip or run his fingers through my hair but he didn't. He kept his distance and would barely even look me in the eye. I knew it was hard for him. It was hard for me and I was the one who was seeing someone else. I was the one who was supposed to be happy.

Brian came to Westville for New Year's Eve. We stayed in and watched the countdown on TV. It felt wrong having him there in the world I came from. It was good for him to spend time with my parents and to see where I grew up, like boyfriends are supposed to do, but I felt like he didn't quite fit. He was in the wrong story. Or maybe I was.

I found myself relieved to drive him to the airport on New Year's Day. I could hardly see through the snow when I got back on the road toward Westville. I drove slowly and carefully, trying to figure out why I couldn't let Brian in. I had compartmentalized him with Megan and the drinking, all tied together in some corner of my mind. None of that was the real me. Chase knew the real me. He had all the parts of me that Brian was missing.

I called my parents and told them I was stopping at Meredith's for a while. I called Meredith and told her that if my parents called looking for me, she should tell them that I had just left, and then call me at Chase's and let me know that I was supposedly on my way home, at which point I would leave.

Struck with sudden conviction, I drove as quickly as the bad weather would allow, white knuckles on the wheel. I drove through the swirling and dangerous blizzard straight to Chase's house, where he welcomed me, tired, teary-eyed, and shivering into his warm arms. For those few stolen hours together, we were absolutely blissful. He held me and kissed me and everything was as it should be. I hadn't lost him. He was still here and he felt like home. I could hardly wait for us to be able to sleep in bed together, to brush our teeth together, and to argue over which movie to rent at Blockbuster. I pictured us living in a small apartment in the city with exposed brick walls. We would have a bed on the floor and hardly any other furniture. There would be stacks

FOUR – WORLD WAR THREE

of books and CDs in every corner, and the bed would never be made. There would be so much love in our little life together.

My cell phone rang and propelled me back to reality. My parents had called looking for me, and Brian had been frantically trying to reach me to let me know that the plane had made an emergency landing in East Tennessee because of the storm. He had to stay the night in a hotel near the airport. I felt like a horrible person. My boyfriend was stranded in the snow and I was safe and warm in another man's arms. But I never felt like I was being unfair to Brian. It felt like I was being unfair to Chase and to myself by dating Brian. I was Chase's and he was mine. I knew it should have felt worse than it did, but my happiness from the fact that Chase still loved me kept the guilt at bay.

A letter came and in it, Chase called me Kim. He said he didn't think this was a good idea, that it should be all or nothing and we had chosen nothing. He was right, we had—I had—yet I was hurt. Even after what had happened on New Year's Day, he was not willing to let me in and if he wouldn't have me back, I might as well stay with Brian. If Chase wasn't right for me, I would find a way to move on.

I rationalized that I was just being a silly little girl, thinking love was something sweeping and magical. I figured this was the way things were supposed to be and it was about time I grew up and thought logically about my future.

February 2002.

It was Valentine's Day. I hadn't been feeling well that week so I was napping after class when Brian came in and woke me up.

"Hey baby! I have something for you. Open this in a few minutes, okay?" He put a card on my desk and he left.

I was groggy from a deep sleep and had to force myself to get up and put on a sweatshirt. I opened the card, which said how much he loved me and to meet him in the Business Center. I brought the card with me and made my way across campus.

The school building was dark and quiet. I looked around the lobby thinking Brian would be waiting there for me but instead there was another card telling me to go to the fourth floor.

I reached the 4th floor and found a card leading me to the classroom where we had first met. The card he had taped to the classroom door said to knock. I knocked twice. I could tell through the small window in the wooden door that the room was lit by candles. Brian opened the door revealing the classroom sprinkled with rose petals. Music was playing on a

FOUR – WORLD WAR THREE

stereo and Brian was holding a red box. I started shaking. He had me open the box, in which a black velvet ring box sat on a bed of more rose petals. Suddenly he was on his knee and he was saying something to me but I couldn't hear the words.

"Yes!" I said.

I believed my own lies.

March, 2002.

I went to Atlanta to meet Brian's parents and I learned a lot that I didn't know about him. He had grown up in the smallest house I had ever seen, filled with tons of junk that had accumulated years of dust and had no purpose of which to speak. No wonder he planned to be a millionaire and subscribed to luxury car and boat magazines.

His parents were fond of me and were very kind, but I never knew what to say to them or what to ask them about themselves. They lived so differently from how I grew up and from how I would want to live someday. *These are going to be my in-laws*, I told myself. *You'll get more comfortable with them.* I ignored my inner voice for a second time and headed back to Nashville with Brian, staring at the shiny ring on my finger.

The pastor at River had been encouraging new attendees to meet with one of the Church's appointed spiritual guides to do one-on-one studies. I wanted to grow in my knowledge of the Bible and to strengthen my faith, so I asked to be paired up with someone.

Coincidentally, I had met my guide before. Her name was Holly. Paul had introduced me to her on one of my earlier visits to Nashville. Once a week I went to her house to study *The River Book*, which is a Bible study book created by the church. Holly taught me the importance of memorizing scripture, about spiritual gifts and, generally, about getting closer to God.

"Picture God on one plane," she said one day, holding her palm out flat. "And you're on another. And sin is the space in between. As you sin, the space between you and God becomes more vast."

I believed what she said was true but it bothered me how I always felt like Holly knew something about me that I didn't want her to know. It was like she was trying to tell me how awful I was without mentioning it straight out. I felt guilty about nothing in particular when I met with her. I was so ashamed of my own heart.

Finally, it was time for Membership class, the final step to becoming a member of River. Megan and I signed up

FOUR – WORLD WAR THREE

and went on a sunny but chilly spring Saturday, Bibles and River Books in hand.

The teacher spoke about the values the church viewed as important, the goals we should each have and the spiritual gifts God gave us. I had talked a little bit with Holly about speaking in tongues and felt that, although the church encouraged it, the idea wasn't necessarily something I saw happening for me. The notion of speaking in tongues was brand new to me and so far from anything I had experienced as a Catholic.

At the end of class, the teacher asked the leaders to lay hands on the new members. The leaders began speaking in tongues and many of the new members, who only moments before had been sitting around me, wide-eyed and taking notes, began speaking in tongues too. One of the men threw up his hands and yelled "Shundalah!" over and over.

I stayed in my seat and listened to the people pray over me. I prayed to myself, *God, thank you for your wonderful gifts. Thank you for your unending love and grace. But I don't know why I'm in this room.*

When the praying and shouting ended, many of the new members were teary from their experience and were eagerly sharing their excitement with each other. Megan and I ducked out the door, walked as fast as we could without running down the hall, got into the car and drove home. The only thing we had to say to each other was, "I think we should find a new church."

One sunny afternoon I was laying in the dark living room watching *Cruel Intentions*, which I hadn't seen in a while. Megan was at class. We only had different schedules occasionally. We waited tables together at a barbecue restaurant downtown, we took most of the same classes, and we went to all the same parties. We had even started dressing alike or as I believed, she started dressing like me. It was always me who would first adopt a particular style and she would pick out something similar. Then we would step out in our matching jeans and solid-colored V-neck shirts from *Express*. I had encouraged it in the beginning, enjoyed being looked up to, but it was starting to bother me. It seemed like she couldn't do anything without my initiating it or without my permission.

I remembered a recent conversation with Brittany, our neighbor:

"Megan asked me if I thought she was prettier than you," she told me with a look on her face that clearly said this amused her.

"Really?" I replied. I was surprised. What an odd thing to ask someone. "What did you say?" I asked. It didn't matter to me what Brittany had said but I was curious.

FOUR – WORLD WAR THREE

"Well, I said yes but that's not the truth." We laughed.

I wonder why she was asking that. What difference does it make? She's pretty! Why does it matter who's prettier? I thought, feeling suddenly glad to have the apartment to myself for a little while. I turned my attention back to the TV.

In the movie, Annette finds out that Sebastian slept with her to win a bet and she left to get away from him and from her humiliation. What she doesn't know is that, despite the bet, he had fallen madly in love with her. He goes from place to place to try to find her, ending up at a train station. This is a big moment in the movie. Annette is riding up the escalator and Sebastian is waiting there at the top. As he comes into view, there is this beautiful, slow, sad piano music playing.

I am colorblind.
Coffee black and egg white.
Pull me out from inside.
I am ready, I am ready, I am fine.

Who is that? I know this song. This means something to me, I thought. *Why do I know this song?*

I bolted from the couch to my bedroom and half-sat on the chair at my computer, typing, "I am colorblind" into a Yahoo! search.

The fourth result down read "Counting Crows Lyrics Colorblind I am colorblind..."

The wheels on my chair slipped from the uneven balance of me sitting on the very edge of it, and the chair crashed to the ground. I barely caught myself before hitting the floor after it. Running on adrenaline now, I grabbed my car keys and wallet and drove like a maniac to The Great Escape, Nashville's best known used music store.

Counting Crows were Chase's favorite band. I had to have that song. I needed to know what it was saying to me.

I found the C's in the pop/rock section and checked the song list on the back of each CD for "Colorblind." There it was, on an album called "This Desert Life." The man on the cover was wearing a black suit and a Charlie Chaplin hat. He had a fish bowl for a head and two goldfish for eyes. I paid $8.99 plus tax and had the CD playing in my car before I even put on my seatbelt.

"I am covered in skin," the melancholy voice said to me. "No one gets to come in. Pull me out from inside. I am folded, and unfolded, and unfolding, I am colorblind." My heart screamed, *Chase! Where are you, what have I done!* The voice sang on, "I am ready, I am ready, I am fine. I am fine, I am fine, I am fine."

I played it again.

I was not fine.

FOUR – WORLD WAR THREE

I got home and put it in the pink stereo on my bookshelf headboard. I played it again. Then again, and again. I sobbed on my bed until my pillowcase, printed in pink kisses, was covered in tears and black mascara streaks. I let the whole CD play on repeat until I was in love with Adam Duritz and Chase and my head hurt and I finally fell asleep.

Something changed in me then. The dam made of all my lies broke and the water of truth bubbled to the surface. I spent much more time alone. I sat in my pink room listening to *Counting Crows*, *Staind*, *Incubus* and *Our Lady Peace*. Brian had started disappearing for hours at a time, anyway, and Megan was seeing one of Brittany's friends so she wasn't around as much. I swam in thoughts of Chase like a mineral bath, healing and rejuvenating. I began to see myself again, to know myself again.

I didn't know how to get out of what I had so deeply gotten myself into. There was a diamond ring on my finger but when I closed my eyes at night, I didn't see the face of the man who put it there. I saw the face of someone else. It was someone else's hands that I felt on me, someone else's voice in my ear, someone who maybe didn't love me anymore. Did he? Could I undo the damage I'd done? I started to think I was going to have to try.

A few weeks later there was a commercial on TV for Nashville's *River Stages* music festival that would take place during the first weekend in May. The headliners were *No Doubt*, *Incubus* and *Counting Crows*. I almost peed my pants. I persuaded Megan and Brian to come with me to see my new favorite band, though both of them really only listened to country music.

We got to the park and found a spot to sit in the grass. We were on a hill that was level with the stage, which was set up on a river barge. I would be able to look straight on at Adam Duritz as he sang to me and twirled around the stage. The minute the band came out it began to rain, which I felt was more than fitting. I let the drops cool my face. *Water cleanses you know, washes the past away, makes new*, Chase had written to me once.

I sat down for a minute and called him. He said he was excited that I had called but his voice had an unwelcoming tone. I wanted him to know that being at a Counting Crows concert was my way of reaching out for him but I couldn't say the words. I was too scared. I didn't know if I said them that it would even matter to him. I didn't know if I believed our relationship could ever work. It seemed like it wouldn't. Yet I couldn't stay away from him.

Later, the rain had stopped, the stars were out and the night air was cool and damp. The band began to play a song

FOUR – WORLD WAR THREE

that was familiar to me but that was not on the only album of theirs that I had so far. My mind began to race. *I'm sure I listened to this song with Chase. I didn't know this was* Counting Crows. *Why is this song important?* I tried to remember.

All at once you look across a crowded room
To see the way that light attaches to a girl
And it's one more day up in the canyons
And it's one more night in Hollywood...

This is Chase's favorite song. The lyrics are framed on the wall in his bedroom. We fell in love lying underneath them.

I began to see spots and I reached for Megan's arm as my knees buckled. She caught me and helped me gently to the ground. I sat there in a daze. The loud music surrounded me.

If you think that I could be forgiven, I wish you would.

I couldn't hold back the tears. Brian sat down next to me but didn't even try to touch me. He had to know what was happening. I felt bad for him but I was too wrapped up in my own sadness to do anything about it.

I had to give him some sort of explanation for what was happening to me. On days when it was at its worst, I told him that I missed Chase, just someone who had been important to me in the past and that I knew it would pass soon. It was no big deal. I wanted so badly for that to be the truth. I didn't want to hurt anyone.

The thing about secrets is that they can hurt you more than the person you're keeping them from. It's like eating the last piece of caramel candy, a delicacy for you alone to experience. You hold it on your tongue, savoring the layers of salty sweetness. It makes you so happy while it rots your teeth.

At least I'd opened up the lines of communication with Chase again. But where would that get us? Could Chase and I make it work so far apart? Would he even be able to forgive me? I became more open about my feelings for Chase. He needed to know how I felt. I needed to know if he could still feel the same.

His letters showed he was as torn as I had been.

```
May 6, 2002 "Let your dim light shine"
Kit, hello hello.  I think its nice to be
back in contact with you becoz' the happi-
est I can ever remember myself being wasn't
while I was partying or laughing with
```

FOUR – WORLD WAR THREE

friends, listening to Our Lady Peace, or watching the muppets. It's when I was with you. When we could both just shut the fuck up and listen to the other one breathe.

I really don't know what to do. I know I still want you, and I know I still love you, as much as that may scare me, the heart wants what it wants, ya know. Maybe no one does understand how we feel. Maybe no one ever will. At some point though, we will and that's all that matters, if you ask me.

"So I memorize the color of your eyes, as you lay half asleep beside me, and I memorize the way our legs intwine as you drift away beside me. I miss waking up beside you..."

May 30, 2002
Kit - Hey, After I got off the phone with you, I just felt like I wanted to say more. I don't know what I'm doing. I think you and I are both smart enough to know that things will never be like that magical summer when we spent all day laying in bed and

falling in love. But that's ok. I can honestly say that I still think about you, and it still hurts that you're not mine anymore. You were everything I always wanted, and of course, I still love you. So that that didn't go to your head, I love lots of things. I love bacon, and I love muppets. I love sleeping and I love escalators. When I was done talking with you, I went and wrote. I haven't written in a long time. There's been no...inspiration. I haven't felt like I've had something to say. I still don't, but now I feel a little bit more like I have someone to listen to it.
I want you to know that my arms are not wide open waiting for you, they are crossed...and I am skeptical. That's just me. Something needs to be proven or done, or something. I dunno.
"You saved me, I hate you. You drain me, I love you. You hurt me, so I hurt you. But now, what do we do?"
Shine.

FOUR – WORLD WAR THREE

It was okay with me that he was protecting himself. There was no need for him to always be unconditionally available. That was a fair move for him to make, but he was wrong; someone else didn't understand me better than he did.

June, 2002.

I knew now, even without any guarantees from Chase, that it was time to let Brian go. The last thing I had wanted was to hurt him. We sat on the steps outside my apartment building, the cement leaving impressions on my thighs where my shorts ended.

"I can't marry you. This was too much, too fast. It's not something I'm ready for." I told him. "I'm so sorry."

"Do you need more time? I'm not in a hurry. We can keep seeing each other," he pleaded. "I love you."

"I'm sorry," I said. "We want different things. We really do."

I gave him the ring back.

He called a few times to ask me to dinner or to come over and talk but there wasn't any point to that. I didn't see him the same way anymore. I couldn't even consider that a relationship with him might be the right thing.

I called Chase to tell him that my engagement was off and that I wanted to be with him again. He was hesitant, understandably, after what I had put him through. He was starting college in the fall, and despite our feelings for each other, I knew all too well that the idea of being single and available to meet new people and experience new things was enticing to say the least. So we stayed in limbo, having feelings for each other but not able to commit. It was what I had been trying to avoid when I left for college, this living in between, but now it seemed like the best of our options.

A week after classes ended, Megan called me from home in North Carolina to tell me that she wasn't coming back. At first I was shocked and angry. I felt abandoned. I berated her in my mind for giving up on Nashville and her country music dreams. However, the more I thought about it, the more I recognized that she had been unhappy. She'd gained weight, allowed herself to be mistreated by the guy she was dating and was otherwise on a constant search for approval. Still, I was heartbroken to lose my best friend.

Fortunately, Belmont did my dirty work when it came to Brian. He was still trying to win me back when he was busted for stealing computers and musical instruments from other students on campus and was promptly kicked out of school. It turned out that's where he had been late at night

FOUR – WORLD WAR THREE

when he would disappear and not answer his phone: stealing things and selling them. *Is that how he planned to become a millionaire?* I wondered, disgusted. Until then, I had still been listening to his pleading because I felt guilty for the way I had treated him, for shutting him out of my heart but when he was forced to leave, I was free from all those feelings. He was not a good guy. He was not someone I should have been with in the first place. I had treated him badly too, but I now felt somewhat relieved of my guilt.

Being devastated by losing Megan didn't last very long when I started to realize how unhappy we had both been. It wasn't the fault of one of us over the other. A friendship founded on need and dependence rather than love and support, even with the best intentions, is bound to be self-destructive. We had been toxic for each other. I felt angry with her but I knew she blamed me for the same things. I knew I would be a reminder to her of a painful year in her life and of how her dream had crumbled under her feet. For all those reasons, instead of apologizing, instead of fighting for her, I let her go. I was getting pretty good at closing my heart to people.

I had spent a year trying hard not to hear my own voice. Now, I was on my own, and I had nowhere else to look but within. I knew I wasn't a victim. It was my own actions that resulted in the pain I felt, my own choices that caused others to hurt. It was time to face myself as an adult. I was alone but I wasn't afraid of it. I saw opportunity. I saw a clean slate, but what kind of relationships did I want to build? Who did I want to become?

I wasn't sure yet.

5
The Air On Fire

August, 2002.

As I entered into my junior year, I considered it a fresh start. I moved into a different apartment on campus with Anna, who had been my Resident Assistant freshman year. I knew she was more conservative than many of the other students—she was still an R.A. and had to enforce the rules. I thought that might be good for me, as a different side of myself came back when I was with Anna. I was responsible, put-together and faithful—not just sad, drunk and confused.

Chase and I had been going back and forth about what to do. He was starting his freshman year of college an hour from Westville. I knew it was unfair of me to ask for a commitment after I had broken up with him in order to have the freedom of a freshman year to myself; for this reason, we stayed in limbo, loving each other but questioning our future together. We both continued to hurt and continued to hope at the same time.

He wrote that even with obstacles in the way, he'd rather die trying to have the one he wants than live a long life with just "someone." He said, "I guess that's how you know it's love." He explained that when he wasn't talking to me it was because he couldn't stand knowing I wasn't his. I was relieved to know it hadn't been out of anger or resentment. He said it was easier to just ignore the problem. "Out of sight, out of mind, right? No, just out of sight."

I told him I would come to see him over the fall break if he wanted. He said he liked the idea and that it tickled him. He said he was afraid I wouldn't be attracted to him.

Push, pull, look away, pull, push.

```
August 3, 2002 "Just a whisper"
I'm as confused as ever, on what or who I
want.
But I miss you. Even when you were around I
missed you. I will miss you when I fall
asleep and I will miss you when I wake up.
```

FIVE – THE AIR ON FIRE

It's love. I'm tired. I wish I was still trying to pursue something in music. It's terrible. It's like there's this evil monster behind my skin, but he can't get out. Don't get me wrong, I love theatre, but sometimes I feel like the only reason I wanna do anything at all anymore is just to spite the people who don't think I'll make anything out of life...or maybe I am just tired.
I love.
Shine.

    I knew that turning away from him had been a mistake and I vowed to myself that I would not make it again. If we weren't going to be together, it wouldn't be my decision. But we weren't together and I didn't know if we would be soon or ever, and so I also vowed to myself that although I was waiting for him in a sense, I would do my best to be open to the possibility of living a life aside from him, whether for a little while or for always.

    I continued to live as if my heart were detached from my body—my heart was at college in Pennsylvania, on stage with him. My heart was in a blue room in the summer, watching movies in his arms. My heart was in an apartment with brick walls in the city, misting rain out the window, sharing my life with him. In Tennessee, I had school and maybe a few friends. I didn't know what else but I kept reminding myself to be open minded.

The only people I was hanging out with were Anna, occasionally Brittany and friends of Brian's. Now that Brian was gone, his friends all showed up to tell me that they'd always liked me and that they were glad he was gone because they had known what trouble he was, and they took me in like big brothers. I would sit on the couch at Ethan's while they smoked pot. They never pressured me to have any. Instead, they just let me know I was welcome to if I wanted. They didn't care how late I stayed over or how much of their liquor I drank. They gave me a good contrast from life at home with Anna. I needed both atmospheres—one to propel me forward and another in which to hide.

One night we were hanging out on the back patio at Ethan's, which was a slab of cement that met a steep hill. I was curled up in an orange velvet chair that sat just outside the door and the guys were standing on the only patch of level grass, smoking cigarettes. I picked at the fuzz on my sweatpants and half-listened to their conversation about drumheads, upcoming recitals and good weed.

"Dude, that blueberry shit was awesome."

FIVE – THE AIR ON FIRE

"Yeah, we'll get some more."

"Anyone want to go to Guitar Center with me tomorrow?" Several of my friends were music majors and they were preparing for upcoming junior recitals.

"I have class and then I work," I said, even though they probably weren't asking me. Why would I need to go to Guitar Center?

I looked at each of the new friends that surrounded me. Kyle was protective—a big teddy bear of a guy, the one who had first reached out to me once Brian was gone. Peter was the artist, weird and interesting with whom I had great philosophical conversations that I mostly bullshitted my way through. Ethan was the sexy one. He had long dark hair and played the drums and his only outfit was jeans and a plain white t-shirt. There was this particular way he would look at me that made my heart speed up. I watched him a little too closely sometimes.

Though I wouldn't commit myself to another man like I had with Brian, I still craved the attention of a man. I wasn't getting enough from Chase. Maybe that man could be Ethan. He was certainly someone who wasn't looking for a commitment either.

"Who wants beer?"

Ethan went inside to stock up for the group.

As Ethan went into the kitchen, two guys came out the neighboring door onto the patio to smoke a cigarette.

I was suddenly hyper-aware of the fact that I was the only girl hanging out with a group of stoner guys and I wondered what these neighbors thought of me. My days of being quiet, friendly, "country music Kim" were over. I liked what I was learning about myself but I was scared that when people looked into my eyes they could see the pain that lay behind them. Eyes are windows and the rooms inside of me were different now.

Ethan came back out with an armful of beers. He offered one to each of the guys. In the orange chair, I tucked my feet underneath my legs and chatted a little with the neighbor guys without taking my attention fully away from the other chatter on the patio.

Ethan never led the conversation. He interjected only when he truly had something to say. Most of the time whatever he said made us laugh, the result of wit and excellent timing. While we were laughing he would chuckle lightly, flash a blinding white smile and run his fingers through his hair, and I would melt.

We all chatted until the bugs began to bite and the group was dwindling. I hadn't realized it was one in the morning and I was disappointed that everyone was leaving. I didn't need sleep - I needed company.

FIVE – THE AIR ON FIRE

Ethan and I went inside. Suddenly eager to fill the silence; he began to tell me about everything he had to do the next day so I sat down next to him on the couch. He was tall, even sitting next to me.

"Hey, just so you know. I'm...I'm really glad you aren't with Brian anymore. I always thought you deserved better." Ethan said with a sudden earnestness.

"Thank you," I said.

Then he kissed me. It was slow, not hungry but rather indulgent. This was a passion born of desire, dark and sweet. I put my fingers in his soft hair and he put his in mine. That was the first night I stayed over at Ethan's, my heart detached.

September, 2002.

Chase wrote that he missed me eternally. He quoted *Counting Crows*. He made a list of things that made him happy: the middle finger he can't give people until they walk away, the feeling he had with the only one he wanted, breaking up a wedding, seeing someone he doesn't know and telling them they're beautiful and having someone ache for him. He said happiness is something that he'd never have again until he had me.

A true artist, the more unhappy he was, the better his creativity. His writing was more beautiful than ever. He was getting lead roles as a freshman at school. But part of a true artist's spirit is that he can't believe that people could believe in him. Furthermore, he couldn't believe in himself.

```
Sept 2, 2002
I miss you, can I say that? I got a lead in
a play, Lysander in Midsummer Nights Dream.
You should come and see it. I wish I still
believed in magic. Who knows?
Cha$e
```

I tried to limit my expectations of him, knowing that he had put a wall between us. I thought it might be made of paper, but it could have been as solid as the brick wall in our apartment in my dreams. It could have been a minefield. I didn't know. Still, we spoke often. He told me a lot about the play, the only thing he was holding onto at school. He told me how much fun he had blocking fight scenes and how they were ahead of schedule and how the director was so pleased.

I made plans to go see him over fall break as I had offered. The closer we got to our visit and to the opening night of his play, the more he began to open up to me and the more optimistic he became.

FIVE – THE AIR ON FIRE

Sept 11, 2002
Kit - Hello. I love you won't you tell me your name, how are you? Are you still gorgeous? I'm sure you are. I'm okay. I don't wanna sound like "the boyfriend" or anything, coz' I know it's not like that, but I really can't wait to see you. Everyone here is tired of listening to me talk about you. They just wanna see you, but not as much as me. Even after all the drama, all the pain and hurt and loneliness, I just wanna see you and hold you and kiss you and have you. Until you leave again.
I love you. "Are you waking up slowly, nothing but lonely, are you waking up holding, holding your breath?"
Chase

Sept 30, 2002
Kit - Hey there sugar pop. I'm so glad you called. I really am. I can't wait to see you. I don't care how many times I have to say that, I will always mean it. I went to the gym again today, but I should stop

telling you I'm getting buff because you're going to expect me to look like someone else, like 98 Degrees or something. I'm sorry, that's not me. But I do love you, to the point where I wanna climb a mountain and tell the world, even if no one was listening, I would still be happy being able to say it.
I like this, this thing where we have feelings for each other, but not like, you know? I dunno, I just love you, and I want you in the rest of my life. Can I keep you?
Shine

    Seeing each other while I was home that fall would be a chance for us to decide what was still there after all of our back-and-forth and if it was enough to save. The pressure built higher and higher as we neared that anticipated week in October.

    I had plans to see *Counting Crows* play at The University of Pittsburgh, stay with Meredith and then drive to see Chase at his school. The concert was amazing; it was even better, probably, than when I had seen them in Nashville.

FIVE – THE AIR ON FIRE

The set was very dark and romantic with lights behind the backdrop that resembled stars in the night sky and giant candelabras on the stage. Adam Duritz sat at the piano or stood at center stage throwing his arms out emotionally as he sang, and I felt more alive than I had in a long, long time.

I heard that the band would sometimes meet fans by their tour bus after shows so Meredith and I circled the arena on foot but we couldn't see the bus. I knew it had to be close by. Then, we spotted an alley blocked off by wooden police barriers and a guard standing on watch.

"Can we go back there?" we asked.

He nodded.

That was it. We were in. A few steps past the barrier, the bus came into view with a small crowd of people hanging out around it. There were maybe twenty or thirty people in the crowd and in the middle, a guy with spiky dreadlocks. My knees began to shake.

I could not believe it. This man had been singing straight to my heart for months now. His words were my feelings. He had led me back to Chase when I had been lost. He spoke for my inner voice when I was silent. I had him to thank for teaching me how deep love could be and that no matter how lost it seems or far away it feels, love is worth it. How could I say that all to him in a moment?

He signed my concert ticket and took a picture with me. Meredith was smiling ear to ear, knowing the importance of the moment she had just captured on my camera.

I said, "You're my hero and I like your coat." It was brown with shearing trim.

He said, "Thanks and I like yours too." I was wearing a gold fur Betsey Johnson coat, one of my first real designer clothing items.

When we got in the car, I screamed at the top of my lungs.

The next day was Saturday. I drove to Chase's college where I found him outside of his dorm building. He hugged me. We were both smiling ear to ear but we were hesitant with each other. It was like someone had handed us each a treasured object that we'd been coveting but that we were afraid might break.

It drizzled all day and the brick buildings looked sad against the gray sky. Chase walked me around the campus introducing me to anyone he knew. "This is Kit, the love of my life."

I saw the school's production of *A Midsummer Night's Dream* that night. Chase played Lysander, one of the main roles. He had to kiss a girl twice, which was hard for me to watch but I was blown away by his acting. Shakespeare isn't

FIVE – THE AIR ON FIRE

easy and he pulled it off with so much charm and so much life.

That night, I showed Chase pictures from school. He loved a Polaroid of me taken at an art benefit in Nashville. The theme had been Moulin Rouge. My dress was black and red with spaghetti straps and a fishtail hemline, and my long blonde hair was wavy, the way he liked it. I wore smoky makeup on my eyes. He liked the picture so much that he wouldn't let me take it home with me. I wrote on the back "Love, your Kitten. Purr."

We kissed each other until we were too tired to keep going. I could still feel him holding back. It was my penance for what I had done to him. All I could do was hope the walls would fall and that I could have all of him again, but I was always leaving and he was tired of watching me walk away. We both knew that I couldn't stay and that he couldn't come with me, but still, we couldn't let go.

It didn't turn out like I'd expected. That love that had remained so strong and waiting under the surface was a mirage. Or maybe we had just done more damage that I'd realized. Once I was back in Nashville, Chase stopped calling or emailing very much, and when I did hear from him, he was extremely distant. I finally confronted him, asking what was going on.

Oct 21, 2002 "Playing with Uranium"
Truth? I don't know how I feel. When you were here, it was good, but I realized that I've changed since we've been together. I don't know what it is, but the spark really isn't there for me any more. I'm sorry. I don't know what that means, but I feel like I should say something. I don't know what any of this means, but yet, I am seeing someone here. I'm sorry, Kit, I'm a dick, but you want the truth so I'm giving it to you. I dunno.
Chase
I love you.

Push, pull, look away.

Could I move on from Chase? I didn't know. It was impossible to say, *oh well, that's that*, and move on. Only time would tell if I really would be able to let go, and for the time being, seeing Ethan suited me fine. It was okay with me that we only hung out late at night and there was usually alcohol involved. Even in the day, even sober, we were cloaked in desire. We didn't tell the guys about us and we were never

FIVE – THE AIR ON FIRE

affectionate in front of them but they all knew it. We had this chemistry that set the air on fire between us. He would look at me from across the room and everyone could feel the heat.

I suspected that he was dating other girls when he would come home late to find me drinking with our friends, his friends. He wouldn't mention where he'd been but he would give me a look that said *don't leave,* and I would stay until everyone else had gone and he would take my hand and lead me back to his bedroom.

I didn't want another boyfriend who wasn't Chase but I wanted love, and I really wanted Ethan. I knew how to enjoy every moment with him; the soft curls of his hair, the darkness in his room, the heat of the alcohol in my blood, his lips on my throat and the pulse of the music on the stereo. *Bat your eyes girl, be otherworldly. Count your blessings. Seduce a stranger. What's so wrong with being happy…?* An Incubus song played while I fell asleep in Ethan's arms.

Incubus had played in Nashville the week before. I went with some of the girls from Betsey Johnson, where I had started working. True to form, I met the tour manager, talked with him about his job and explained that I wanted to be a tour manager too. We exchanged email addresses to keep in touch as I was still pursuing my dream, though I was beginning to forget why.

One cold afternoon, I was slowly making my way home from class. It was dark, though it wasn't even 5 o'clock. I was thinking about how much I hated the lifelessness of winter and that's when my cell phone rang. It was a Westville number that I didn't know.

"Hello?"

"Hi!" said a chirpy female voice.

I was silent and I was filled with a sudden feeling of betrayal and my blood went as cold as their air. It was Crystal.

"How are you? I ran into one of your friends from school and she gave me your number!"

I made a mental note to find out who it was and scold her.

"Hi. I'm good. Just headed home from class."

I didn't know what to say. This was not someone I wanted back in my life, not now or ever. Even the sound of her voice from hundreds of miles away made me feel like an insignificant little girl, weak and naive. She told me about how she was racing horses in Ohio. I listened and responded on command but I made no comments at all about my life. She couldn't have even one piece of me anymore. I would not let her do more damage to me. I ended the conversation politely, knowing I'd never answer another call from that number.

FIVE – THE AIR ON FIRE

you make me feel about me. With you I'm smart and beautiful and say (some) things worth saying. And I love the way you make me feel about the world. It's at my fingertips when you're at my side. I don't fear the distance. I don't even fear your uncertainty. We're a tank. We're more meant to be than Romeo and Juliet. (We get to live.) There's no way God would let me feel like this if you weren't going to come around. I'll give this to you when you do. To say thanks and I believed in us all along. I love you. Kit.

While I was writing love letters to him that I wouldn't send, he was sending letters to me that were void of love. His mood was flat. I couldn't decide if I was pleased that he wasn't being hateful or if I was disappointed that he wasn't being romantic. We were in purgatory, trapped between a heaven and a hell of our own making, waiting for something to change. Something, but who knew what? Certainly not us.

December 19, 2003
Hey there. How are things? I'm back at school. It's going ok. I wish I had more

to say. I wish inspiration would just come to me. It's happened before when songs would just come to me, like I wrote it all at once. Now there's just fragments and choruses. I don't wanna write recycled songs. Oh well, things could be worse. It's good to have you in my life. Know that. I don't know what to say about romance or what's gonna happen. But I do know that much.
"I was in bed with a girl at the end of the world, and she said I'm going home..."
me

December 21, 2003
Kit - Hello, how are you? I wanted to write. I dunno, I just felt like it. So, I dunno if you knew this but whatever was going on between me and Becca has been completely over for quite some time. She kinda just said it's done, and I was like...O. Then I found out she and one of my friends hooked up when they were on a trip this week, and I was like, O. Whatev-

FIVE – THE AIR ON FIRE

```
er.  Well, I guess that's it.  I'll talk to
you later.
name
```

And so I just kept writing to myself.

My birthday that semester had been an evidence of my failures in creating meaningful relationships. I invited all my guy friends to my party as well as Anna and the girls from Betsey Johnson. I wore a red dress, a color I didn't often wear because of its boldness. I chose Hamilton's, my favorite Nashville restaurant, for dinner. It was warm for November so I sat on the screened patio under an outdoor heater and enjoyed the fresh air. I knew my server from frequenting the place. He brought me a French martini while I waited for my friends, even though I was only turning twenty.

Anna had to babysit—she had told me a few days earlier—so I knew she wasn't going to make it. She said we would do something special later. People were always late, it seemed, but when ten minutes had gone by I called Kyle to see where he and the guys were.

"Oh, we'll stop by later, where is it again?" I knew then that they wouldn't show.

I called Brittany but she didn't answer.

By then I didn't even feel like calling any of the girls I worked with. I should have known they wouldn't come. They were sweet but completely unreliable.

Happy birthday to me.

How did I get here, celebrating my birthday on my own? How had I managed to alienate everyone in my life, to isolate myself by choosing people who gave me only so much of themselves and to whom I gave only so much of myself? Was this a method of protection? Was I scared of being hurt? Was I afraid to keep hurting other people? All I knew for sure was that I was really, truly alone.

6
The Edge of Sanity

January, 2003.

I hadn't seen much of Ethan after spring semester began and I found out why one afternoon when Kyle came to see me at my apartment. He acted like he was just stopping by, making small talk at first but when he managed to work into the conversation that Ethan was seeing someone, I knew that was why he had come over. Kyle was the unfortunate messenger.

I wished I'd been able to walk away on my own strength but at least I finally had the push I needed to emotionally step away from Ethan. I turned some other things around that spring too. Chase emailed sometimes but it was always small talk about what shows he was doing or if he'd played at an open mic night lately. He stopped calling me Kit. I hated it but at least I wasn't crying over him and I was sleeping in my own bed most of the time. I wasn't drinking. I was studying, managing a band at school, writing a lot and getting a proper amount of sleep at night.

I even found myself praying rather than avoiding the shame of my brokenness.

Dear God, please set my watch to your time. Help me be patient and let you remain in control of my life. Thank you, Lord, for loving me and for sending your only son, Jesus Christ, to die to save us from our sins. You give me so much more than I deserve Lord and I praise you and love you and give you my life. Over and over again.

God, remember how Chase used to completely adore me? He loved the way I breathed, he loved my hair, he loved it all. I want that again. I want someone to think I'm a dream. I think I deserve that. I'm like a split personality; I'm okay and so not okay at the same time. There's a war in the Middle East and a war in my soul. I'd love for both to end peacefully and with minimal casualties.

There were times when I thought of Chase more than others. Times when I would dream of him, feeling him lie next to me when I turned out the light, feeling his hand hold mine and feeling him kiss me. I'd been dreaming of our dream—our cool bare apartment. The dreams were peaceful,

SIX – THE EDGE OF SANITY

not desperate, not full of sadness. I still believed it could happen.

I had left my white jacket at Ethan's the last time I was over there. I wore that jacket often enough to miss it so I had to get it back. On the afternoon I dropped by to pick it up, I could hear music playing so loud that I had to pound on the door to get him to hear it. He opened the door and gave me that gigantic electric smile; it was the smile that he used when he wanted only one thing, the smile that made me trip over nothing trying to get out the door—if I even made it out the door at all.

"Hey! To what do I owe this pleasure?" he greeted me.

"Just stopping by to see if you had a jacket of mine here."

"Oh, sure! How are you?" He let me in the door past him. "You look great."

Suddenly I felt like I was in a wolf's den. I had to get out before he could sink his teeth in to me.

"I'm good thanks. Here it is! I gotta run but I'll see you..." I didn't want to say "soon."

"Cool, yeah, I'll call you..." I was gone before he could finish, waved quickly from the sidewalk as I hurried toward home.

Finally, jacket in hand, I had learned to make it out the door.

May, 2003.

I went to Las Vegas with Service Corps to work at the Academy of Country Music Awards and the related press events. During some downtime, I explored the city with Lacey, a girl I met on the trip. I had kind of a girl crush on her right away, from the first moment I saw her as I was jumping into the van that would take us from the airport to the hotel. She was beautiful, though I don't think she knew it, and she was wearing the prettiest navy and cream skirt. I was in awe of her wardrobe throughout the whole trip and as I got to know her, I liked her a lot as a person too. Both of us were often quiet when we were in a group of students, but when left to our own devices, we had plenty to talk about. We started to become friends.

The day of the awards, I saw a lot of my old friends as I was volunteering on the red carpet. Each volunteer was assigned to an artist or "talent" as they were called; we were to escort them between press interviews much like what I had done at the Country Radio Seminar. The TV host was there as well as the eldest from the band of brothers and a newly signed artist who I knew from my days spent waitressing

SIX – THE EDGE OF SANITY

downtown. He played in the house band at the restaurant where I used to work and the song that I always requested turned out to be one of his hits.

Although I was the only student to already have friends in this world and I liked thinking that maybe I had a leg up on the others, I was still willing to put in the work as a volunteer. I knew I had a lot to learn and a long way to go to build a career.

"Hey! Where are you interning this summer?" Lacey asked, coming up beside me as we waited to be assigned to the next wave of arriving talent.

"A PR firm, you?" I asked.

"A management company. One of their artists has a big annual event so I'll mostly be helping with that. Gosh, her dress is gor-geous!"

"It is!" I said and then she was off down the carpet with another artist.

As the pre-show wound down, I was buzzing with excitement. I loved the energy of live events far more than any studio or office work I'd done. The flashbulbs on the carpet, the electricity in the air and the slight sense of urgency backstage, it all turned me on. I was completely infatuated.

Over the summer, I started my first internship for Belmont, filing news clippings for a PR firm that did publicity for several major country music acts. I also modeled for a photo shoot with a coworker at Betsey Johnson who was trying to build her portfolio as a photographer. The best part had been choosing the outfits I'd wear, and in what scenes I'd be wearing them: black and electric pink sitting in an old car; a blue tank and jeans, legs in the pool (jeans and all); a soft white blouse on a bare mattress in a peach colored room; a white miniskirt and jean jacket in front of a wall splashed with graffiti. Putting the visuals together, the color, texture, and mood came as naturally to me as understanding the world of music. I started to wonder if this might be a direction to explore, something having to do with helping the artist create an image. I'd have to learn more about that side of the business.

While we were shooting, the photographer put on some music that caught my attention. The woman's voice was sometimes clear and sometimes gritty. She sang words that were so poetic and yet painted such an honest picture of real life: a poor small town girl, friends lost, broken love. "A wind that blows as cold as it gets blew out the light in my soul," she sang. Her name was Patty Griffin. The photographer let me borrow the CD but I bought my own copy almost right away. I had that familiar feeling of deeply connecting to songs, being moved by the beauty of a melody and finding peace in the company of words.

SIX – THE EDGE OF SANITY

June, 2003.

A group of old high school friends were going to a Dave Matthews Band concert and camping in Pittsburgh. I drove up to join them, having heard what fun they'd had the year before. I wore ripped jeans and a white tank with green polka dots, styled my blonde hair straight and looked in the mirror for a moment before we loaded the car. I didn't look particularly different from the way that I had being in high school, yet there was something that made me feel like I stood out a little more. I had been so plain before but I couldn't quite put a finger on what might be different. Maybe it was just confidence or maybe it was all in my head.

Jeff Meyers was there and he hardly recognized me. It may have been because he was wasted by the time we found the guys or maybe it was because he didn't expect me to be there since I lived so far away. I had been hoping he would be there, knowing he was a DMB fan from our days in biology class where I sat behind him staring at the band logo on the back of his hoodie.

"Kim Carlson!" he shouted, finally figuring out who I was. "What are you doing here? It's so good to see you!"

He showed a lot of enthusiasm for someone who hadn't really ever been my friend to begin with but I beamed and let him hug me tightly. We talked for a few minutes about what I had been up to, which always sounded amazing when I summarized: "I go to school for music business. I want to be a tour manager. I was in Vegas for an award show last month..." It was just life to me but getting to explain it to someone outside of that world, even I became freshly excited by it.

"What about you?" I asked.

"I'm at school in Ohio, studying art. I want to be a museum curator or something like that."

I smiled at him, my eyes huge with awe, though I would have thought it was cool if he had said he wanted to be a museum janitor. Everything he did was cool. I kept an eye on him all night but I found that I was able to just relax and be myself and enjoy the music and the evening with friends. For a short time, I was able to set aside the monitor that I always seemed to have focused on what others might be thinking of me. I let myself forget my worry about what was going to happen with Chase or when I might finally be who I was hoping to become. Who I was now was enough and that felt good.

I considered the trip a success and headed back to Nashville, where I was still working at Betsey Johnson. I had a great manager who was helping me become a better sales person and I was really enjoying learning about fashion. We

SIX – THE EDGE OF SANITY

put on a fashion show at a club downtown that was a huge success.

One day, I was filmed for a show on CMT with my TV host friend helping a girl pick her dress for a red carpet event. She had won a contest to attend the event with her favorite artist. We set it up so that the cameras would watch her come into the store and I greeted her. She told me about the contest and what she was hoping to wear and I helped her pick out some things to try on. Then, she purchased her favorite item, a long black dress with purple ruffles at the bottom. They even filmed me talking to the camera about Betsey Johnson and why that dress was the best choice for their contest winner.

When the show aired, I picked myself apart. Why did I wear that shirt? The camera does add ten pounds. And I talked way too fast. I still loved it - I would just have to do better next time.

Senior year of college began that fall. Anna had graduated so I moved off campus into an apartment with Brittany. We would go downtown to the dance clubs twice a week, dressed in pinstriped pants or jeans, tank tops or corsets and dance until three a.m. Then, since I was underage and had had much less to drink, I would drive her car home and she would roll down the window and demand we go through the McDonald's drive-through.

"Pleeeeease Kim!" She yelled, leaning out the window with her blonde hair wild in the wind.

"I'm so tired, can't we just go home? You don't want McDonald's anyway. You know you'll regret it tomorrow."

"Please please please!"

I got in the left turning lane and signaled.

The mornings that followed, I would sleep in till noon. I had some hard and uninteresting classes that semester. Instead of rising to the challenge, I found it easier to go to class only as many times as was required of me.

Living with Brittany was difficult. She had a boyfriend who she suspected was cheating on her and who was always yelling at her and taking advantage of her kindness. He went to school forty minutes away and didn't have a car so she drove him all over middle Tennessee. He didn't have money so she bought him food.

I knew she cared about me but in reality she was dealing with some serious issues, and since she was older and had a dominating personality, I found myself believing and agreeing with everything she said. She taught me that food was the enemy so I ate green beans all the time, until I couldn't take it anymore and would gorge on pizza. She would say, "Skinny feels better than food tastes," as she made lunch out of a rice cake.

SIX – THE EDGE OF SANITY

November, 2003.

One Tuesday night, I was at home with Brittany watching TV.

"Let's order pizza! Would you eat some pizza?" she asked.

"Okay," I said, "but no regrets. This is a treat and I'm not going to feel guilty about it."

I thought we'd eat the pizza, watch a movie and enjoy a quiet evening at home. Wrong. She swallowed three pieces and left me alone with some stupid show on TV. I felt like a complete cow, and the guilt that would have been avoided had this truly been a treat of an evening began to creep in.

Not knowing if Brittany was asleep, I turned the shower on so she wouldn't hear me, though she probably would have cheered me on, and I stuck my finger down my throat. It was hard to do, which surprised me, and I only got a little bit of the pizza to come up. I went to bed with pizza still in me, thinking I could feel it making me fat. It felt like poison.

Trying to follow in her footsteps, I was supposed to have two to three no-food days that week and I had failed, so to make up for it I didn't eat anything till my birthday the following Sunday. The most frustrating thing was that it didn't seem to make a difference. I still looked the same in my clothes. The numbers didn't change when I stepped on the scale. My dissatisfaction with myself was a tricky little thing. As soon as I learned to fight him in one form, he would morph into something else.

Despite the cutting, the drinking and the fasting, I could never call myself a cutter, an alcoholic or a sufferer of an eating disorder. The times when I was trying out different types of destructive behavior were just that: trials. I don't know if it was my faith, my sense of responsibility to my parents, a guardian angel, or something else, but despite the many moments when I walked to the edge of sanity, I never jumped.

I started seeing a therapist at school. I told him I was worried about money. This was an issue I had never had to deal with before. I wasn't spoiled by any means but we had never had to worry. I was about to go to Belmont West in L.A. for a semester and I knew I wasn't going to have a job and I was going to have to rely on my parents. That is why I was working all the extra jobs but I couldn't hold onto the money.

We talked about Brittany and about how I wanted to save her from her troubles, and how I was trying to encourage her with little success to drop the boyfriend, to finish school and to drink less. I was afraid to keep repeating friendship patterns from my past, like the negative influence

SIX – THE EDGE OF SANITY

from Crystal or the codependency I had with Megan. I wanted things to be different with Brittany. He told me I could be her friend but beyond that I had to let it go, and that it was up to her what she did with my encouragement.

There were so many other things I should have talked to the therapist about but I couldn't bring myself to say those things out loud. I found it impossible to admit to my own struggles. It was much harder to see myself for who I really was when I was so busy criticizing myself for not being who I wanted to be.

December, 2003.

One rainy day just before Christmas, I found myself listening to "This Desert Life," the *Counting Crows* album that had caused a pivot in my life a few years back. It had become my favorite album of all time. It made me feel—just, feel. As always, after a couple of songs, I wanted to call Chase as I longed to hear his voice.

There would never be enough people to talk to about him. I wished for someone who would listen to me read all his letters and tell all his stories. I could close my eyes and remember walking into that theatre in the marketplace, hearing him say, "Dry your eyes, Kitten." I could feel him holding my hand and I could feel his pillow on my cheek. I hoped he knew that he was the love of my life and that when I thought of pure happiness, I thought of him; that when I thought of heartbreak, I thought of him and that when I dreamed, I dreamed of him. I wondered if he knew how badly I wanted to be with him.

One Sunday I went to my new church with Lacey and cried three times throughout the service. I felt like God was putting a spotlight on me that said, "Bad person." I looked at all the people looking at me and I mentally dropped to my knees and said, "Yes, I am sorry." I felt that I had taken such advantage of God's love. I was holding His hand and kicking Him in the shins at the same time, and it wasn't working. I was supposed to hold His hand and walk with Him. I wanted to love Him, to live in His will and in His future. I wondered why I was wasting time.

Dad came to Nashville to help me pack up my stuff to keep in storage while I was in L.A. Brittany's stuff was already gone, back home in Ohio where she was headed to get a clean start. Dad painted the walls in our apartment from the blues and purples to white. It was strange walking through the empty apartment. My battered purple room was gone; Brittany's bruised blue was gone. Two coats covered everything and it was like none of it had ever happened.

SIX – THE EDGE OF SANITY

I stayed with Lacey for a few nights while I had my last round of final exams. One night, I hung out with Ethan, Kyle and the guys who I hadn't seen in so long. It was easy for me to be around Ethan now; he was just one of the guys to me. I shared some of my bottle of Crown with them and for the first time, I took a few hits off of their pipe.

I went to the bathroom and stared at the polka dotted shower curtain for a few minutes. *I wonder if I can count all the dots,* I thought. *One, two, three, four...* I got to about fourteen before I lost track and started over. Finally realizing that I was high, I giggled at myself in the mirror and went back downstairs. We played our own game of TRL where I was me and Ethan was Carson Daly and the others were audience members. I was so glad for a chance to have laughter pour out of me again.

Before I left Nashville, I wrote some letters to say goodbye. I never sent them but it helped me to close some of the chapters in my life. I had some anger, disappointment, and regret that I needed to let go of and to truly get away from.

To Megan, I wrote that she had broken my heart. She had abandoned me. I would always kind of hate her for that. I didn't understand how she could wake up and say, "I don't want my best friend anymore." Still, I believed I was better off without her. Spitefully, I wished she could understand that. I also wrote that I was sorry for my part in it all. Despite my negative feelings toward her, I knew that her negative feelings toward me were well deserved. I closed by writing that I hoped she'd see me on TV someday and say, "Damn, I could be doing that too but I gave up. Kim is awesome." I detested the way she abandoned her dreams. *Goodbye, Megan.*

To Brian I wrote that I knew I'd hurt him but he'd been lying to me all along too. I really hated him, but I also wrote that I hated myself for wasting so much of my time not being honest with either of us. He did bad things and he lied, then he got caught and so he told new lies, and there was no limit to whom he would lie. I had lied too, but I'm the one who came clean in the end, I argued. *I'm glad you're gone.*

To Ethan I wrote that I was sorry to him and to God for whatever had happened between us. I was sorry I let my moments of low self-esteem or selfishness, or both, take over my good judgment. I was sad for him that he was selfish enough to take advantage of women. I felt lucky to have escaped knowing that my God is forgiving. I hoped he'd learn that too before it was too late. I hoped that he wouldn't raise sons to treat girls like he did. *I'm letting go. Goodbye.*

To Anna, Brittany, and Lacey, I wrote that they were the people who made my college experience in Nashville so much fun. Whether I'd known them from the beginning like Anna or I had met them more recently like Lacey, I knew they'd always be in my heart and I hoped I would be in theirs too. I wrote that they were all such vibrant and inspiring people and such valued friends. I wished them love, happiness and the realization of all their dreams. *With love, Kimberly.*

I packed them all away in my journal, the people and my sins, and wondered when I would find something that I wouldn't have to leave, I wouldn't try to run away from, and I wouldn't need to say goodbye to. Was this pattern something I was choosing because I was afraid of settling? Was it a pattern I could break? I used to fall asleep imagining what I would become, but now I fell asleep worrying about what was wrong with me.

Maybe L.A. would fix it.

January, 2004.

On New Year's Eve, I flew to L.A. to start the Belmont West program. There were fifteen of us in the program and we would all live in the same apartment complex. My internship was in the Music Supervision and Publishing department at a major film company, and my jobs were to select music for the movies that the studio was working on at the time, and to monitor the publishing for songs that they owned. The latter consisted mostly of filing and faxing but for the former I got to watch the dailies (what had been filmed on set each day), make notes and research potential music for particular scenes.

I spent a lot of my downtime lounging by the pool in my hot pink bikini, listening to Pearl Jam on my headphones at full blast or hanging out with the other students. We planned group outings to places like the Holocaust Museum, The Crystal Cathedral and some of the hottest restaurants in town, even if all we could afford was a martini and a shared appetizer. We had parties at any one of our apartments, playing cards or watching movies. We went to see live tapings of TV shows like *Leno* and *That 70's Show*. An old music star from the 70's was one of our neighbors and we got to hang out with him a couple of times. He had some friends who were younger musicians and we would all sit around listening to their music, the old star praising them and dancing around the room. Through Service Corps, I also got to work the red carpet at the Grammy Awards.

I met some guys from San Diego at a *Dave Matthews* show. I went to visit them in San Diego a few times and I got to work with their band a little, booking a couple shows for them. Since my discovery of *Counting Crows* and the love for rock music that followed, I had begun to think of living in L.A.

SIX – THE EDGE OF SANITY

rather than Nashville in order to be part of the music scene. I planned to come back to L.A. after my last few summer classes at Belmont and continue working at the movie studio. I would get an apartment with some of the other students who planned to stay and keep learning the ropes of the industry. I also started looking into acting schools, thinking it would be fun to take a few classes.

Chase and I continued the occasional emails, usually punishing each other for our own failures. I told him over and over about the plans I had and the new bands I liked that made me more like him. He was sarcastic and self-deprecating and I felt guilty for making him that way, though I wondered, was it entirely my fault? I couldn't get my head around the idea that Chase wasn't the one but I kept trying to meet others, knowing that if he wasn't then someone else was bound to be.

Still he kept writing to me.

```
Jan 18, 2004    "The Memory of the Fish"
Hello.   How  are  you  doing?    I'm  ok.    I'm
lying.   I'm  actually  pretty  depressed  and  I
don't  know  why.    Perhaps  I'm  just  lonely
and I  wish  there  was  a  girl  in  my  life,  or
maybe  I  just  hate  school,  who  knows.    I
```

apologize, Kit, I realize none of this is your fault. I hope things in L.A. are glitzy and exciting. Don't spend ALL your time schmoozing with the stars. I wish I could use that word more in conversation...schmoozing.

Anyway, take care of yourself. Stay happy and beautiful.

Take pains, be perfect -Shakespeare.

Chase

June, 2004.

After Belmont West was over, I spent three weeks or so in P.A. because I was about to graduate college and would soon join the work force in one way or another. I wanted to spend some quality time with friends and family who I didn't get to see me very often.

I planned my time at home to include the *Dave Matthews Band* show at which I had had so much fun the year before. Meredith and I went to the campgrounds with our other girlfriends from high school to set up the tent. Actually, the girls sat and chatted while the guys set up both tents. The year before, we had waited until after the concert to set

SIX – THE EDGE OF SANITY

up camp, but it was dark and we were drunk and it was a complete disaster. This year we knew better.

Once we got to the amphitheater, there was less time to tailgate than usual but we had enough time to get a decent buzz. I wore dark Seven A-Pocket jeans and a hot pink tank top. We were able to find some of the other Westville people including Jeff Meyers just before the band started. Meredith and Rachel left to get more beers from the overpriced concession stands, and the rest of us talked and swayed and sang along. I was ignoring Jeff as I was not going to keep trying to flirt with him forever.

Eventually, I caught his eye and said "hi," but left it at that. He had grown a beard and cut his dark hair short, making him look even more striking than ever. I smiled to myself.

"You should really do something about that," one of the girls, Amy, said to me, referring to Jeff.

"I am done wishing for that," I said. "It's just never going to happen."

"I don't know," Amy argued. "Maybe you just need to make a move."

Amy had dated Jeff in high school and had nothing good to say about him as a boyfriend, but they had managed to stay friends and she never criticized my crush.

"Well, if I were to make a move exactly how would I do that?" I asked.

"Just grab him and start dancing!"

It sounded insane but what else was I supposed to do? Meredith wasn't back yet to give me her advice. *What is taking them so long? Hmm. Maybe...*

I turned and smiled at Jeff; then I reached out my hand and said, "Come here!"

He smiled and came over to me. I was standing about three steps down the hill. He could tell that I wasn't trying to have a chat. He put his arm around my waist, resting his hand on my lower back and we swayed our hips to the music. I reached up and put my arms around him and he pulled me closer. I glanced at Amy and she was smiling.

Jeff kissed my neck and then kissed me on the lips. My mind went completely blank. I was lost in the moment, the music and the deep slow kiss. When I finally came out of it, Meredith was standing next to me, holding her beer. I laughed. I knew I would have to explain later, but at that moment, there was no way I was letting go of him.

We danced and kissed through the entire show. Jeff got increasingly drunk and he would stumble down the hill a little and I would hold on to him to keep him from falling. We would laugh.

"Where are you sleeping tonight?" he asked.

"I don't know yet."

"You should stay with me."

SIX – THE EDGE OF SANITY

"We'll see," I said. I wasn't considering turning him down, I just didn't believe he was seriously inviting me.

It took us forever to get back to the cars after the show. We were all hopelessly drunk on alcohol and euphoria. Once we finally found the cars, we were in no hurry to leave. The traffic was barely moving to get out of the parking lot anyway.

The guys had a bottle of Jagermeister in their trunk. We took turns taking swigs straight from the bottle. I always thought Jager would be hard to get down but it wasn't. It tasted like black licorice, which I didn't like but at least it didn't taste like the ridiculously strong alcohol it is.

There were too many of us to sit normally in the car, so I sat on Jeff's lap, sideways, so I could turn and see him. I was still smiling, staring into his dark eyes. It was then that I was able to take a few minutes to realize that I had kissed Jeff Meyers, and that he had asked me repeatedly to stay with him that night. I didn't care that he didn't love me. I didn't care that we were drunk. All I wanted with him was a moment.

When we got to the campground, we started a fire and got out the snacks; no one was tired yet. We were all completely amped. Some people got marshmallows out and held them over the fire on metal sticks. When I went to sit on the table, I put my hands behind me to pull myself up and accidentally rested one of my hands directly on a hot metal stick. I heard my hand sizzle first and then I felt it. I was too drunk to react quickly and by the time I finally moved my hand there was a decent burn on my palm at the base of my thumb. Some of Jeff's friends had seen it happen. I was so embarrassed but I assured them that I was fine and that it wasn't a big deal. Really, it hurt so badly I knew that I would cry in a matter of seconds.

"Come on," Jeff said. He took my good hand and walked me across the dirt path to where his Jeep was parked. I wondered if anyone had ointment or a bandage or something. Jeff had a pipe and some pot. *Well, that might help*, I thought. We each took only a hit and Jeff said, "Come on, let's go find somewhere else." I buckled my seatbelt even though I knew we were only driving around the campground. It was dark and we were in no state to drive. I even had visions of us careening off a steep hill, hitting every tree as we rolled down.

He drove around for a few minutes until we were lost. Finally, we found an empty camp spot and parked the Jeep.

"We can sleep here."

Jeff put the seats down in the back and laid out some blankets, making a bed. We climbed in.

My memory went as dark as the summer night's sky.

SIX – THE EDGE OF SANITY

The next morning when I woke, it took me a few minutes to figure out where I was. Then I remembered: the concert, Jeff, kissing, Jager in the parking lot, campgrounds, Jeep...Oh. My. Gosh.

My eyes flew open. There he was, next to me.

Jeff stirred.

"Hey," he said, pulling me close to him. "That was fun, we'll have to do it again sometime when I'm not so drunk and I can enjoy it more."

I was too shocked to respond in decipherable English.

We stretched our cramped legs, stiff from sleeping in such a small space, and climbed to the front. SUVs may have ample cargo space but they are not better than a tent.

"Great, now we have to find where everyone else is," Jeff said. Of course neither of us remembered exactly how we got to where we were.

He backed the jeep out of our spot and drove about thirty feet before we noticed a few familiar cars and some early risers we recognized a few camp spots down. All that driving and we had somehow managed to sleep at a neighboring camp spot. Meredith had to be up and back to her house early that morning so Jeff and Jesse drove me back to her place. We got on the highway and Jeff turned on the stereo. He had an *Incubus* CD in.

"I love *Incubus*," I said. "A friend of mine is their tour manager."

"No way," Jesse said.

"That's awesome. I can't imagine meeting famous people like you do," Jeff added.

"Yeah, they're playing in Nashville again this fall. You guys should come down for the show." I have a habit of inviting people to do everything. Sometimes I need to just shut up.

"Oh my gosh, that would be awesome," Jeff said. "What do you do that you get to meet all of these people? I mean, I know you're in music somehow."

"Um, I just finished up a semester in L.A. doing music supervision for a film studio, which is choosing music for movies, and getting all the proper licenses and stuff. Now I'm about to graduate and I'll be back and forth between L.A. and Nashville this summer." It was true, after my time at home I was going back to L.A. to find a job and an apartment, then I would be in Nashville again in August for graduation.

"That's so cool," Jeff said.

"You're in Ohio, right?" I asked Jeff. "How's that going?"

He had changed his major to history.

I found it amazing that all the years I had had such a crush on him, and yet we knew very little about each other. I asked Jeff and Jesse both questions about their schools, their lives and I told them some more of my own stories, trying to fit the best stuff into one car ride without sounding like a name dropper.

We eventually made it to Meredith's house. I thanked her for not minding that I didn't stay with her or ride home with her.

"I would never stand in the way of that!" she said. "Now, tell me all about it!"

I told her what I could remember and we laughed about how she had made her way back to us at the concert to find Dave's tongue down my throat.

"Ims," she giggled, using her special nickname for me, "I had no warning at all!"

I remembered my burnt hand. Meredith offered me some ointment and a bandage but it didn't hurt very badly and I decided I wouldn't mind if it scarred so I passed on her offer. I could use a permanent memory of that evening.

The next day I drove to Westville. Chase and I had emailed a few times while I was in L.A. but things were really weird with us. We both admitted that we still had feelings for each other but he was either cruel or cold most of the time.

I figured I deserved it, although the worst I had ever done to him was break up with him. Twice. The desire to be with him fueled many of my decisions. I wanted so badly for him to be in love with me again, though I believed he still was deep down. Although his *I'm so happy for you* statements were dripping with sarcasm, I thought he strived to impress me too, in his own way.

I got ready to go to his house with great care. I wore a little blue Jim Morrison t-shirt, my dark A-pocket jeans, and white pointy-toed heels. Rock and Roll. I scrunched my long blonde hair so it looked like I had beach waves. California girl.

I was so nervous when I knocked on his door. He answered and I walked into his wonderland, the rabbits and the birds all saying *hello, welcome home.*

His mom was there and she asked me all about school and California. I could tell by her questions that Chase had been talking to her a lot about me. Could it be that he was proud and not just angry?

We talked for hours. We did end up lying down on the bed and watching part of a movie but he never touched me except for hugging me hello and goodbye, and I didn't stay very late. These last few visits we had both been so hesitant with every movement and every word, like if we touched each other we might turn to dust, like if we talked about our feelings we might spontaneously combust.

7
Tumbleweed

July, 2004.

It was almost time to graduate college and move to L.A. and I couldn't wait! I may not have had the celeb-studded pool and all the free time like I had at Belmont West, but I preferred to be busy anyway. I would be working and making a name for myself doing something like managing bands. I would find some new friends and settle into a small but charming apartment. I imagined that I would wear sweet colorful A-line skirts and tanks and carry a Louis Vuitton, spending weekends on the beach riding bikes and getting a tan. First, I had to focus on my last two classes before my new life could start.

Because I was only going to be in Nashville for a month, I stayed with Lacey and her roommates instead of getting an apartment. When no one else was home, I would sing Julie Roberts' songs. *Oh the things lovers do when it's over. Oh the things lovers do when it's done. Find a cool bottle or a warm shoulder, wake up older and try to move on.* I sang to the bathroom mirror, an earphone in one ear while the other dangled below my shoulder.

My car was still in L.A. so I had to walk everywhere or get a ride. I felt stranded. It was too hot to walk anywhere.; every day was over a hundred degrees. Kyle and Ethan were living in a house across the street from Belmont and I went over to visit a few times. I hung out with Lacey and her roommates a little bit. They were really great Christian women and I wanted to be more like them. I wanted to feel like I was really a part of their group but no matter how nice they were to me I knew I would always be an outsider. When I compared myself to them I felt so dirty and damaged. They had a way of making me feel lucky to be around them. I studied their clothes and their vocabulary. When I first became friends with Lacey, she taught me which brands of jeans I should be wearing and when I got my first $170 pair of Paper Denim and Cloth jeans, they all joked, "You're in the club now!" But I wasn't, really, and I wasn't in Ethan and Kyle's club either for that matter.

SEVEN - TUMBLEWEED

One day I called Anna to let her know I was back in Nashville, and she invited me to come out to her new boyfriend's pool about twenty minutes outside of town. She was already out there so she asked a friend that she worked with at Starbucks, Sophie, to pick me up on her way out there. Sophie was also from the Pittsburgh area and Anna was excited for us to meet. She told me Sophie would be there to get me at 11:00. I got my suit on and packed a beach bag, and then I waited outside until a little black car pulled up.

"Hi," she said. "You must be Kim?"

She had shoulder length light brown hair and tanned, olive skin. She was tiny with cheekbones to envy and eyes the color of burnt honey. I told her where I was from and that I was about to graduate. She told me that she still had one year left as a commercial voice major. *Everyone's a singer*, I thought. But she had Julie Roberts' CD playing so at least she had taste.

It was great to see Anna and it turned out that Sophie and I had a lot in common. We talked about home and we talked about boys. She seemed to say whatever she thought without concern for what I might think. Whether she was self-assured or just honest I didn't know but I found it refreshing. She was funny and she reacted to what I would say in a way that made me feel heard. She was smart and interesting and I think she thought I was too. *Maybe Sophie and I are in the same club*, I thought.

The first week of July I flew back to L.A. It was great to have my car again but I still didn't have a job or an apartment. Well, I kind of had a job. The movie studio had agreed to take me on as a temp; they would call me on days when they needed my help in various departments. The first few days I was in L.A., I had nothing to do so I spent money that I didn't have at the Beverly Center Mall and watched a lot of movies at the house where I was staying on a previous Belmont West girl's couch. She lived in a one-room pool house off Pico Boulevard at a house with no pool.

Finally, the movie studio called and said they needed me the next day to fill in for the VP's assistant. *Well, that's one way to start,* I thought. I was only slightly nervous to be filling such big shoes. Luckily, it wasn't a day when anything major was happening. I answered the phone and took messages or let her know what or when her next appointment was. I thought it was very exciting to see the idea boards that documented who might play the leads in upcoming films. There was a different air on this floor compared with the music supervision department where I'd interned. Music people are super laid back but everything had a feeling of

SEVEN - TUMBLEWEED

importance here. I couldn't decide if I liked the high-pressure environment or the laid-back atmosphere better.

The president's assistant sat in a cubicle next to mine, where I could only see the top of his head over the cubicle wall. We talked a little bit over the office IM. He told me he played a small role in Cruel Intentions II, which I never saw. *Everyone in Nashville is a singer. Everyone in LA is an actor. What am I?*

I tossed and turned again on the couch that night. It was hot but that didn't matter. I would have been awake anyway. Something had been off ever since I got back to L.A., but I had no other plan. *I have nowhere to go. Nashville? What would I do in Nashville?* I turned over again and wrestled with the blanket, kicking it off one leg. If I were to be working at the movie studio or anywhere, I would be working very, very hard with long hours, high stress and very little free time; it would be a while before I was even in a position that I enjoyed. Would I love this work or this town enough for it to be worth it? I was afraid that I didn't. I couldn't afford to live here if I worked in retail. I didn't have a lot of friends in the city. The only real friends I had made at Belmont West were either back in Nashville or south of L.A., in Huntington Beach or in San Diego.

My mind continued to spin: The extra twenty pounds I'd gained had me feeling insecure, traffic in L.A. was ridiculous, I kept getting parking tickets because I didn't understand the parking signs and everything was so expensive. I was beginning to hate the city, which surprised me. Finally I fell into a hot, restless sleep.

I woke up the next morning and called Anna in Nashville. She had mentioned that she wanted to move to an apartment in the complex where her boyfriend lived, where we had gone swimming with Sophie. Apartments in that area were affordable on any budget. I could work a retail job in Nashville and still pay my bills until I figured out where to start to get to where I wanted to be. I had friends there who wanted me around. Anna was thrilled when I told her that I was considering coming back and living with her.

Next I called Dad to tell him I wanted to go home to Nashville. I think he was relieved but he never said that. He just said, "Okay, whatever you want to do is fine with me."

I began to pack the car to drive three days by myself back to Nashville. I gave myself one day to take care of everything that I needed to take care of and I would leave the next day.

On day one of the drive, I saw my first dome sky. The world was so flat that I could see the level horizon all around me and the sky looked like a dome. Skies like that will give you perspective when nothing else will. The second day, a tumbleweed blew across the interstate. *I'm in a western mov-*

SEVEN - TUMBLEWEED

ie, I said to myself, laughing. I found it so much easier to laugh now that this weight had been lifted from my shoulders. That night I stayed in Albuquerque and had dinner at an Applebee's near the hotel. I was truly enjoying being on my own without any plans other than to follow Interstate 40 East.

The third day my old rock star neighbor from L.A. called.

"I just haven't seen you around lately," he said, "so I thought I'd call and see how you were."

"I'm great, thanks. I left in May but I was back there last week."

"And where do you live the rest of the time?"

"Nashville."

"Well that's great," he said. "You take care and let me know when you're in town again."

"I will!"

I can't believe he just called me, I told myself. *Your life is weird.*

A week later I found out he died in his L.A. apartment.

Life really is weird.

August, 2004.

Anna and I moved into our apartment a week before graduation. Everything I owned except for what I had in my car was in storage. My parents were planning to bring it all with them when they came up for graduation. I slept on my bedroom floor until then. *At least I have a home now.*

My favorite thing about the apartment was my walk-in closet. It was deep and had so much space that I could organize my clothing like I had been taught at Betsey Johnson: light colors to dark, lighter fabrics to heavier, sleeveless to long-sleeved. Sometimes, I would lay on the floor in my closet and look up at the variety of fabrics and colors above me. Each one so unique, coming together to create a collection that described me in all the ways I can be seen. Some days I wore a hot pink T-shirt and ripped jeans, another day I was in a black dress with thin straps and lace trim across the skirt. Sometimes, it was brown boots with cropped tweed pants and a deep turquoise satin camisole.

I got a job in retail. Betsey Johnson had replaced me and didn't have an open spot but there was a store that was moving to a new space in the mall and wanted extra help. The manager was by-the-book and very good at what she did. I liked her right away, though I was a little scared of her too. She lived and breathed her job. I've always had so much respect for people with that kind of passion. I became the pant expert, familiar with every fit, every fabric and every color. I could look at a customer and tell her not only which fit would flatter her figure but which size would fit best and what we had available.

I hated what I had to wear to work. I had worn clothes from the store in high school and college and was tired of them. After Betsey Johnson, these clothes were vanilla compared to Chunky Monkey; classic, sure, but bland. Better mixed with other things. My personal style was developing just as my personality was. Even just a little, I was becoming surer of both.

Things were starting to go a little better now that I was feeling settled. I had Anna, an old friend by now, and then there was Lacey, with whom I was going to the same young church we'd found before I went to L.A. She was also my shopping buddy and the only friend I would share clothes with. However, Sophie was becoming my closest friend. It seemed that she was everything I had been searching for.

Sophie was the best singer I'd heard at Belmont and that's saying a lot. There are some seriously talented people at Belmont. Sophie could sing anything and make it sound like her own, as though the melody had been written for her voice alone and the lyrics from her own life. We spent a lot of our time the same ways, reading and listening to music. We always had so much to talk about between our favorite bands, the guys we were interested in and our goals for the future.

Sophie moved out to our neighborhood, across the complex from the place I shared with Anna. I took her to her first *Dave Matthews Band* concert. We watched all of the Steelers football games together. Our lives aligned so easily.

I stopped in at Betsey Johnson one day that fall and chatted with one of the girls that I had worked with there before. She told me they were hiring part time. She scheduled me for an interview with Lily, the manager that I had loved working for, and within minutes of the interview Lily hired me back.

Since the position was only part time, I needed something else. I couldn't work at both stores due to conflict of interest rules so Anna got me a job at Starbucks where I got to work with her and Sophie. I trained alongside Jen, another new girl. We tasted all kinds of coffees and espressos. I could tell the difference in the flavors—one nutty, another one with a hint of berry—but I didn't enjoy the taste of any of them. I preferred the Chai lattes and caramel macchiatos.

I didn't quite know where my life was going but now that I'd decided to live in Nashville and I had an apartment and a job, I felt much more at ease with whatever direction my life might take from there. I wasn't lost anymore. Even if I didn't know where I was going, I knew where I was starting from.

September, 2004.

Now that Chase wasn't in school and was considering moving out of PA, it seemed the first realistic opportunity we had for a future together. We still wanted the same things: an artists' life in the city, brick walls and our love. I decided this was the time to really go for it and if we couldn't make it work this time, then I was going to have to let go.

I was at home, painting flowers on a new canvas—my newest hobby—when I decided on a bold romantic gesture. I painted "I'm Still In Love With You" on a piece of notebook paper and balanced it between the wings of the angel statue he'd given me so many years before. I took a picture, uploaded it to my new laptop and emailed it to him with the subject, "Just a Note..."

```
Sept 23 "Not Just a Note"
Kit - That means so much to me. What a
breath of fresh air, thank you. I was look-
ing through pics yesterday (cleaning) and
```

saw my box of notes from you. It was then that I realized how I had fucked up by letting you go. I'm trying to clean up and going to narcotics anonymous meetings a lot, and it's nice becoz' feelings are coming out again and inspirations as well. Unfortunately, or hopefully fortunately, I'm also still very much in love with you. I was walking the other day and I saw a lil statue, not as cool as the one I got you, but it made me miss you. I absolutely want "this" to go somewhere. I don't know what to say right now coz' there's so much distance between us, ya know? But I do love you and I can't stop thinking about you. A great thing about you is how you make me feel about myself. I feel like I've been wasting my time since we've been apart. It was truly magical when we were together, at least I'd like to think so and I'd love to get that back. I dunno, I don't really know what to say. I'm kinda nervous to be honest with you, but I think that's a good thing. I love you.

Take pains, be perfect...

SEVEN - TUMBLEWEED

Shakespeare

Narcotics anonymous? I had known he smoked pot with friends sometimes, but I didn't think it was that serious. I wondered if this was just a new way for him to try and fix himself. Regardless, it seemed that my bold gesture was worth it. I couldn't imagine my life with anyone else. Who else would understand me from the glitter to the grit and appreciate all of it? Who else would I see for all the cracks in his heart, the battle of hope against hopelessness that he was always fighting? Who else would fight alongside him like I would?

For just a moment, it looked like all of this believing in love was about to pay off. Then a cold wind blew out my candle.

Oct 1, 2004

So I don't even know what I'm doing right now, Kit. Jana and I broke up not even ten days ago, and to be perfectly honest, I'm still grieving and I'm not emotionally or physically ready to jump into something else. I'm an emotional wreck, and even though I know in my head how much better you are for me and how good and right and

encouraging and hopeful and positive you are, I don't know if I can be what you want me to be right now. Yes, I do still have feelings for you, but I don't know in what capacity. I feel like shit doing this to you, becoz' I know you don't deserve it, and I feel even worse that I didn't have the balls to tell you this over the phone...but I guess that goes to show even more what kind of person I am. I am sorry, but I couldn't go on holding this in much longer. Please don't hate me too much. I will talk to you soon.
Chase

Well, that was it. He hadn't even said he'd been dating anyone in the first place. Now I knew that it was time to move on. We were far more separated that I ever wanted to believe. I had loved him more than anyone else, but it was over now. I didn't know how to believe that it wasn't him. I didn't know how to even begin to picture myself with someone else. I didn't know if I could let anyone else in. But I was going to have to try.

I threw his framed picture off my balcony just to hear my heart break.

SEVEN - TUMBLEWEED

One rainy November afternoon I was sitting at Starbucks reading a book. I wasn't scheduled to work that day, but since I had become friends with a lot of the baristas it was fun to just go and hang out, plus it was a great day for a good book.

Jen came to sit with me on her break.

"What are you reading?"

"*White Oleander*," I said, "my favorite book. I read it every year."

"It's that good?"

"Unbelievably."

"Cool. I'm bored. We've been slow today. Hey, what are you doing this weekend? It's my birthday Friday so I'm going out to Virago with some people."

"Yeah, Anna told me," I replied. "I think we're planning to come."

"Good. There's actually this guy who's going to be there that I think you should meet."

"Does he like *Counting Crows* and *Dave Matthews Band*?" I asked.

"Yes!"

"Okay, then."

Jen told me his name was Chad. She had been very good friends with him since they were kids. She said he was a good guy, a very good guitar player and a good kisser. I thought it was strange that she wanted me to go out with a guy she had kissed but she insisted it was weird when they kissed because they were such good friends so it didn't matter.

For Jen's party, I attempted a combined style of preppy and rock and roll, wearing ripped jeans and a Kurt Cobain t-shirt with a pink cable knit sweater and heels. Chad was wearing a collared shirt and tie under a v-neck sweater with jeans. He had a goatee and wire rimmed glasses. He was very tall with dark hair. I thought that he looked like Tom Hanks. Lipscomb guys were different than Belmont guys. He was more clean-cut than my usual "type," but I could use a good guy for once.

"Hey, I'm Chad," he said in a full, warm voice. I shook his hand.

"Kimberly. Nice to meet you."

He invited me to sit by him on the low booth seat in the lounge near Jen's other friends.

"So you work with Jen at Starbucks?"

SEVEN - TUMBLEWEED

"Yeah we trained there together but I just put in my notice. I also work at Betsey Johnson and they have a full time position available for me."

"Full time job? Are you still in school?"

"I graduated from Belmont in August."

"Oh, that's nice. I'm a senior at Lipscomb. I took a year off so I should be done already and I'm so ready to be done," he said.

"What's your major?"

"I'm a psychology major so I'll probably end up in grad school eventually."

"Oh no, more school? You're already over it!" We laughed.

"Not right away. I play guitar in a band so maybe I'll be able to do that for a while. I don't know. We'll see. What about you?"

"I was a music business major and I want to be a tour manager," I told him.

"Oh, very cool!"

He was nice enough, but he seemed so educated and proper. He would never get a tattoo. He would never smoke a cigarette. He would never be exciting enough to keep me interested, but he would never break my heart.

Love as a Cliff

November, 2004.

A few days later, Sophie and I were working an evening shift when Chad came in. He ordered a triple Venti latte, which in Starbucks language meant a drink with three shots of espresso. *I guess even the good guys have their drug*, I thought. He thanked me for the drink and asked if I had a break coming up, then he sat at an empty table in the cafe. Good posture, wire-rimmed glasses and a neatly trimmed goatee.

"That's the guy Jen's trying to fix me up with," I whispered to Sophie. We made faces at each other and giggled. She and I generally liked the same kind of guys. Guitars, tattoos and a few days post-shower—probably a few days pre-shower too, for that matter. I thought Chat was cute, I just wasn't sure if I could be attracted to him. I think he'd showered too recently.

On my break, I left my green apron on a hook in the back room and went to sit with him. My white polo had espresso stains on it and my ugly brown shoes were splashed with milk. I felt disgusting, but was I really trying to impress this guy?

We talked about music, about his band practice, about my work in fashion and what life had been like in L.A. He was smart but not pretentious, which I found refreshing. It was an easy conversation. I realized we did have a lot in common and Jen was right about that. We liked a lot of the same music. He liked *Dave Matthews* as much as me, if not more, and that was very important to me.

The next night Jen called and asked Anna and me to meet her and Chad at a new pizza place in town. *She's determined*, I thought. However, after my conversation with him at Starbucks, I was starting to think that he might be worth spending some time with.

I had been trying to learn how to ask a guy about church when we first met to get that out of the way. Maybe that would keep me from getting into relationships where faith was such an issue like with Chase, like with everyone.

Chad belonged to a denomination called Church of Christ, which I didn't know much about, but he was a Christian so that was good enough for me.

"Do you...?" he asked.

"No."

Somehow I knew he was going to ask if I went to church every week, which I don't. One of the great things about not being Catholic anymore was that I was allowed to miss church without the guilt.

"For me, there's more to faith than church," I told him.

"I totally agree," he said. "So you were raised Catholic? Why did you decide to leave the Catholic Church?"

"It is too based on rules. You must be in church. You must memorize these twenty prayers. You must hold your hands properly when you take communion. I do think there's some beauty in the tradition, but I wanted to find a church that focused on a relationship with God, that celebrated His love, that moved me to tears every week in humility of His grace and power."

"Wow," Chad said. "I know exactly what that feels like. Church of Christ is very rule-based too, but there are some things about it I really like. We don't use instruments in church, which seems a little weird but everyone singing together a capella is so amazing."

EIGHT – LOVE AS A CLIFF

I liked him. No one else at the table was paying any attention to us anymore nor were we to them.

"Have you read *The Quarterlife Crisis*?" he asked.

"Yes, I hated it," I responded, knowing myself well enough to know the material in that book didn't apply to me, and being comfortable enough to be upfront with him.

"Why?" he asked.

"Well, I always know what I want and I go for it," I replied, "and if I change my mind, that's fine, but I'm never at a loss for what's next and I don't believe anything is unattainable."

"I could have guessed. I can tell you are the opposite of the people in the book."

I was astonished. This guy could see right through me.

"This is the most intelligent conversation I've had in a long time," he said.

Usually with guys I didn't always feel like I came across as particularly intelligent but we were spanning some serious topics: religion, books, art and music. I was used to being the drunk girl in her bra, and found this to be a nice change of pace.

Suddenly, I became very aware that I wanted him to kiss me. I never make the first move, and in this instance, neither did he. He did ask to see me again, though we figured out that we both had busy weeks. I had afternoon shifts at

Starbucks and he had morning classes and band practices at night. The next time we would be able to see each other would be a week later at my birthday party.

The next day, he called on his way to band practice.

"I just thought I'd see if you were going to be up for a while in case I'm not at practice too late," he said.

"Yeah, I don't work early tomorrow so I'll be up. Give me a call."

He called just after midnight.

"I'm not waking you, am I?"

"Not at all," I said, "I was just working on some lyrics."

"You write songs?"

"Just lyrics. I don't play any instruments so I co-write with friends."

"I write music on guitar but I suck at lyrics."

"Maybe you can help me put some music to these!"

He came straight from band practice with his guitar and we sat down on my bedroom floor. The first one I read him was "Willow," which I had written that summer about a girl who makes life decisions by what song is on the radio.

"It's about how seriously music can affect our lives," I explained.

EIGHT – LOVE AS A CLIFF

"I get it," he said. "That's so true. Do you like *Phish*?" He held his guitar as a shield and wouldn't quite look me in the eye. He was scared.

"I like Dave and Trey's stuff, but I don't really know *Phish's* music," I said, referring to collaborations between *Dave Matthews* and *Phish's* front man, Trey Anastasio.

"Well, I like *Phish* even better than Dave. Their music has opened so many doors for the kind of music that my band plays. You'll have to come to our next show!"

He wants to see me again.

We wrote music to three songs that night and talked until 6:00am. I had to convince him to set down the guitar. He seemed unsure of what to do with his hands without it. The longer we talked, the better he became at eye contact. And then he left. He didn't try to stay over. He didn't even try to kiss me.

I fell asleep smiling.

The next day was my first shift back at Betsey Johnson and I went all out, so glad not to be in khakis and brown loafers at Starbucks. I wore a strapless lace cupcake dress that faded from tan to rose to black with black heels. Lily was so glad to have me working more because I was always a big help to her. I was so eager to learn and grow that I took over a lot of her duties like goal setting and schedule making, just for the experience.

I was closing up the store when Chad called and asked if I wanted to meet up with him and some of his friends at a sports bar a few blocks away.

"I'm a tad overdressed," I said, "but if you don't care I don't."

I sat with him at a booth while he and his friends drank foreign beers and I sipped a mixed drink. He held my hand under the table. It was clear from the way his friends talked to me or said, "So nice to meet you," that he had told them about me.

When the group was thinning, we weren't quite ready to end the night.

"Where do you usually hang out?" he asked.

"My favorite place in town is Hamilton's."

"Jen's just getting off work, why don't we have her meet us there?" he asked.

So we did. The three of us closed down the bar, talking more than drinking and when we had nowhere else to go, Chad and I sat in his car in the parking lot and talked until after three a.m.

That is what falling in love is supposed to be like. Sleep no longer matters. You can't risk missing the next

EIGHT – LOVE AS A CLIFF

words out of his mouth. You can't separate yourself from his presence. You can't unlink your fingers from his. Finally, I managed to get out of the car and drive home, sleep settling in just as the euphoria wore off.

I knew I would catch up on sleep that weekend because I was babysitting at the Jamison's house overnight. I had been sitting for them occasionally since sophomore year. Now, Maggie was 10, Peter was 6 and baby Sawyer had just turned 3. I would go to bed shortly after they would and get a decent eight hours of sleep for at least two nights.

Chad called Saturday afternoon.

"How's it going?"

"Ugh! They are great kids," I said, "but the boys fight when they get antsy and the little one cries every time. I need to get them out of the house for a bit so we're going to McDonald's for dinner. Would you like to meet up with us?"

We were already at McDonald's when Chad came in so he said hello then went to order his food. The boys were playing in the colorful plastic tunnels and Maggie and I were talking at a table nearby. A mature ten year old, she and I were able to have real conversations from when I first met her.

"His beard looks like a bird," Maggie said, pointing out the fact that his goatee was indeed sort of shaped like a bird with its wings spread out. I laughed.

He talked to Maggie like I did—like she was a small version of an adult. He listened to her opinions, and I was so impressed. The boys were understandably too busy to care that we had company for dinner, and I was glad they were occupied by something other than wrestling each other for a while.

We left and Maggie told me in the car how nice she thought he was.

I was reading on the couch after I put the kids to bed when Chad called.

"How are they?" he asked.

"Asleep. Sawyer's in his parents' bed. He wouldn't sleep in his own but that's fine."

"What are you doing now?"

"Reading a book about Marilyn Monroe... Would you like to come over?"

"Would that be okay?"

"Yeah, I'm like family. They wouldn't mind. We can watch a movie or something."

I was wearing a black velour tracksuit and my hair was damp and wavy from an evening shower. I added a little mascara as I now cared what he thought, but in a way that still kept me from trying too hard.

EIGHT – LOVE AS A CLIFF

We watched *Shrek 2* and we actually watched the whole movie. The kids may as well have been awake. I was dying for him to kiss me but I still refused to be the one to do it. The movie ended and we talked about other movies we liked.

"My favorite movie of all time is *Playing By Heart*," I told him. "In the opening scene Joan tells Keenan about a friend who once told her 'talking about love is like dancing about architecture.' Her whole monologue about it is amazing. I could do the whole thing but I won't."

But we talked about love.

I told him I was giving him control for two reasons. First, because he told me he had never been in a relationship where he was in control, and he didn't like that because aggressive girls frightened him. Secondly, I had noticed that whenever I started to be the one leading the progression of a relationship, it started to go badly.

Then, Chad turned to me and grabbed both of my hands in his.

"I've been wanting to do this for days and I can't wait any longer."

He put his hand on my cheek and he kissed me. When it was over, I turned back toward the front of the couch and tried to catch my breath and collect my thoughts.

Besides the fact that it was a physically perfect kiss, it shook me to my core emotionally. I blushed red as a rose and I couldn't speak.

Me, with no words. There's a first time for everything.

"Please say something," he said nervously.

But I just couldn't think of the right thing. "It was good" wouldn't do it justice. What I was actually thinking was too scary, not that it wasn't true but to say it out loud would be too much. Finally, I just explained that my silence was a good thing.

What I was actually thinking was that that kiss would be my last first kiss ever.

One of the things that Chad admired about me was my hobby of painting. I had only been painting for a few months and I was entirely self-taught. I didn't really care if anyone thought they were good enough to sell. I just enjoyed being able to express myself. They weren't about other people seeing them.

I never topped the very first one I did. The right side of the canvas was gray, the left side covered in pink and yellow flowers with little black seeds. Scattered on both sides were sharply shaped pieces of black, and the words "and it breaks her heart" were written in spring green over the grayness.

EIGHT – LOVE AS A CLIFF

It was basically a visual of the Dave Matthews song, "Gray Street," where he says, "All the colors mix together to gray and it breaks her heart." The black shards were my broken heart.

Was I finally moving on from Chase? It really couldn't get any worse. He had passed on me repeatedly to date people that he said weren't as good for him as me, but I just couldn't keep hoping that he would come around. Apparently, we weren't going to make it work. And all the colors mix together to gray.

A second one I did shortly after the first was more interesting to Chad. This one had a turquoise background with several mustard yellow lines intersecting across the middle. At two points, the lines held yellow signs, one with an up sign and the other pointing down. In black script I had painted, "I am ready, I am ready, I am fine." Chad didn't know what I meant by the signs, but he knew right away the words were not what they said. He guessed that at the time I had painted the picture I was far from fine; although, I seemed to be doing alright now.

We painted together. I laid the old sheet I used to protect the carpet out on my bedroom floor and put out two fresh canvases, my paints and the brushes. We left the door to the balcony open to get some fresh air circulating in the room and we set out to work, agreeing not to look at each other's work until we were finished.

I was too nervous with him there to focus on my work and I had nothing deep and seriously sad to paint about so I continued to get frustrated and paint over what I had done, and then over it again. Finally, I gave up as he was finishing his piece. He showed it to me.

He had painted a man in different positions: first crawling, then half-crawling/half-walking, then walking, then shielding his eyes, then what looked like being slain and then flat on the floor, dead. All of this was happening in a white bubble inside a blood red border; the caption he used was a cue taken from me and it included the words, "out of the darkness comes light...?" This was a Dave Matthews lyric to which he added a question mark.

The next night we went to dinner with Sophie and her new boyfriend. The guys got along so well that Sophie and I joked that we were intruding on their first date.

They were talking about their musical influences.

"I think the guy learned bass from Jesus," Sophie's boyfriend said about his personal hero.

"Jesus played the bass?" I said. "I *love* that guy!"

Everyone laughed.

EIGHT – LOVE AS A CLIFF

After dinner Chad and I went to his parents' house, where he was living while he finished school. We tried to watch a movie but the giant flat screen TV wouldn't work so we talked instead. I told him that he was charming, and he told me that I was captivating.

"I have this metaphor," I said. "I see love as a cliff. In my experience, when a guy and a girl get to the edge, the girl jumps and the guy hesitates. By the time he thinks he might jump, she's long gone."

"I'm pretty sure I jumped last night," he said, and my heart skipped a beat. "And it's scary!"

"The fall is the best part."

9
an Attainable Future

And we fell.

The night of my birthday party, after blowing out twenty-two candles and saying goodbye to all my friends, Chad and I sat alone at our big booth in the almost empty lounge, talking and kissing like two fools in love. I hadn't made a wish; there was nothing else that I wanted.

That weekend, I went to Pittsburgh to celebrate my birthday with Meredith. She was living in an apartment in an old house in Oakland, one of my favorite areas of the city. I liked walking from her place to Chestnut Street, where there

NINE – AN ATTAINABLE FUTURE

were boutiques, restaurants, a coffee shop and a record store. I talked about Chad the whole time.

We decided to throw my birthday party at Meredith's place so I would have a chance to see the people I wanted to see and drink what I wanted to drink. I invited Chase. He said he would like to come, and he would try to get a car and drive down. Two hours passed and I hadn't heard anything. Good thing I knew not to get my hopes up.

The party—my birthday party—was a bust. There were very few people there who I knew and even fewer who cared that it was my birthday. Chase never showed up. He didn't even call to explain. I had a few drinks and sat quietly on the couch alone. I'm not good at pretending that I'm having fun when I'm not so I went to Meredith's room to lie down.

I thought of all of the dreams that I had with Chase, I thought of our apartment in the city, and I decided to let it all go. Whatever path my life would take was the right path for me. It really was time to move on. I was ready. *I am ready. I am fine.*

I really was.

Back in Nashville, I was in full Chad mode. "I am definitely falling in love," I wrote in my journal. He took me to a party to introduce me to his friends and band mates. Lipscomb students are very political compared to Belmont students. Belmont students choose their friends by creative chemistry. Lipscomb students choose their friends by where your father works or what social club your mother is in.

Regardless of their politics, they seemed to like me. I got smiles and raised eyebrows, and "so you're the girl Chad is dating" comments. We were sitting on the couch in our own little world when a thin girl with curly blonde hair and dimples burst into the room and proclaimed, "You're Chad's girlfriend!" I felt my face get hot and I smiled at her. Then, I looked helplessly at him. "Well, if that's okay with you," he said, "I've been saying that for a few days now."

Yes, that's okay with me.

For Thanksgiving, I cooked the turkey at my apartment and drove it over to Sophie's, where we ate while watching *Steel Magnolias*. Chad came over later that night. We were kissing in my bedroom when he suddenly lifted me off the bed a little and pressed me against the wall. Not violently but playfully. He looked me in the eyes, a mischievous grin pulling the side of lips. Then he kissed me deeply. I was elated and I couldn't get enough of him.

I couldn't wait for what was next, specifically, because I felt like I was ready to have sex with him. I had waited much longer with other boyfriends, some of whom I lost because of it. This was what I imagined an adult relationship was supposed to be like. Still, he wasn't taking things that far.

One Friday night, we went downtown to one of the Nashville's honky-tonk bars and had a few drinks with some of his friends. Later, after the usual round of kissing, I reached for the elastic waistband of his boxers. He moved my hand away and put my arms around him instead. Then, he pulled his face away just enough to look me in the eyes and he said gently, "First the ring, then the thing."

I could not believe it. I had spent the last six years turning guys down or wishing I would, wanting and hoping to wait and the one time I was willing and wanting sex in a relationship, I was told to back the truck up? I felt dirty, I felt hurt and then I was amazed. I was touched that someone saw me as precious and on top of that, I was excited at the idea that this man might just marry me. This amazing, caring, smart, sexy man might marry me.

I met his parents, which was hard to avoid for long because he lived with them. He went to school just a few miles from his parents' house so he planned to live at home until he graduated the following spring in order to save up some money.

They were so nice. Right away, I found them very welcoming and easy to talk to. They reminded me a little of my own parents—if my mom loved cooking and crafts and if my dad carried a highball glass around. He also had an older brother, James, who was applying to law schools. James was extremely proper and educated, always using big words but never being a showoff. We got along particularly well; he took an interest in me and I enjoyed our conversations.

I really fit in with his family and with his life and I was glad he had family values like mine. His parents were still together, involved in church and supportive of his dreams. They were the kind of family that I was looking to be a part of some day. I was finally making the right decisions when it came to love.

I watched myself change, blossoming into a woman in love and discovering not just what I wanted out of life someday but what was actually within my reach. I envisioned us as Chris Robinson and Kate Hudson; he was the quiet classic rock star and she was a beautiful flower child. They had just enough educated hippie and just enough rock and roll, and we were going to be just like them.

I spent a lot of my time with Chad or with Sophie, but I still had Anna and Lacey and groups of other friends too. It was a much healthier situation than I'd been in with Brian and Megan, when we were all so dependent on each other.

I still loved Chase, though it wasn't the same. I had come to accept that things hadn't worked between us, but I did consider him to be the only guy before Chad I had really loved, and I knew it was okay that he would always be special to me. We weren't really speaking but not because we were still punishing each other.

December, 2004

One evening we rented the movie, *Eternal Sunshine of the Spotless Mind*. I thought the theme of the movie was an incredible idea—to erase someone from your memory and to go on living as if they'd never existed. I wondered if I would really go back to who I was before I'd met the person who'd been erased. Or would I always wonder how on earth I'd gotten so into rock music, and why it was that I so adored all things dramatic.

I did move on from Chase, but I didn't erase him. As I reflected on the idea, I decided that no matter what happened, I would never have erase one moment of Chase in my life. He shaped me like he had written me in a song. I breathed life from his words and I danced to his melody. I was thankful for it, and Chad met me there, in a place that I wouldn't have been if it weren't for Chase. And he was falling in love with me, just as I was with him.

One night Chad pointed out a rendering of Nashville's Union Station hotel that was framed above his parent's couch.

"There's a restaurant inside there," he said. "That's where I'm going to propose to you."

He caught me off guard but his statement bothered me for more reasons than just surprise. My mind reeled. *What for? Because it's fancy and expensive? That's not personal. We've never been there before. I have no emotional connection to that place.*

Dad put a ring on Mom's finger one day while she was napping on his couch—sweet, private, personal and unexpected. I just figured that I would let him do his thing. I did believe I was going to marry him, but I also didn't feel that there was any hurry.

Chad was gone over New Year's Eve, recording with his band in Texas. I tried not to miss him. I didn't want to be so vulnerable. I didn't want to need anybody. Sometimes I focused so hard on not being one thing that I put myself in danger of leaning too far in the other direction. Sometimes I forgot that I didn't have to be perfect.

Chad was a wreck without me in Texas. They were in a cabin and he didn't have very good cell phone service so we didn't get to talk very much. When he got back he told me he

NINE – AN ATTAINABLE FUTURE

was lonely and he thought maybe I had found someone else while he was gone. I told him that was ridiculous and he was such a fabulous boyfriend that we could clone him and sell the clones on eBay. He told me that he gave the band guys a heads-up that he was going to be the kind of rock star husband who would need to have his wife on the road with him. I said that was okay with me.

We just knew that this was it. I couldn't believe how my life had changed so quickly and without warning, how what we had just started was bigger than both of us could have imagined.

Over the next few weeks, I got several phone calls from out of town with big news. My first boyfriend's newest girlfriend was pregnant, and Brittany was engaged to her boyfriend in Ohio. College was beginning to feel like it was so long ago. It hadn't even been a year since I had graduated but I was paying my own electric bill and my boyfriend had a key to my apartment. This was definitely a new level of adulthood.

January, 2005.

One colorless winter Friday, I was working at Betsey Johnson when two women walked in. It was a heart-stopping moment as I realized one of them was one of my favorite songwriters of all time. I had just been telling my manager,

Lily, how I was going to see Patty Griffin play the Opry the next night, and having never seen her play live before, I was extraordinarily excited.

There she was in my store, looking at the clothing on my racks. I turned to Lily and whispered the woman's name; my eyes, I'm sure, were bigger than usual. I excused myself to the back room to collect my wits and call Sophie. I was going to get her out of class if I had to. Amazingly, she had just pulled into the mall parking lot. I hung up the phone and took a few deep breaths, and then I went back out to attempt some kind of normalcy while talking to the woman who wrote some of the most genius lyrics I'd ever heard.

> *It's funny how the morning turns a love to shame*
> *Disguised and disfigured*
> *And you thought I tasted like rain*

I had trouble making conversation with her as easily as I would a normal customer. All of a sudden no words came to mind that sounded right in my mouth. She was tiny, fragile and her curly auburn hair seemed to sum her up—untamed and fiery. I did manage to take the dress and jacket she had picked out to the fitting room, and to ask her through the rose printed curtain how she like the outfits. She bought the green Battenberg jacket. As she walked away, Sophie, who had been casually browsing racks, and I beamed at each other. I said a silent prayer that she would wear the jacket at the Opry the next night.

A few nights later, Chad and I were lounging on my bed when we got a call from a friend that Trey Anastasio, lead singer of his favorite band, *Phish*, was at the Tin Roof. To both have a chance to meet our heroes in the same week was unfathomable. We were up and running to Chad's black Jeep within minutes. It was a good fifteen minute drive to the Tin Roof with light traffic. Trey could be anywhere by then but it was worth a try.

The bar was crowded. We made our way to the back room and we saw Trey talking with a few people. Chad and I found a spot to stand near him, where we would be able to speak to him when his conversation with the other folks was over.

When we had our chance to say hello, I introduced myself along with Chad and then stepped back a little to let him have his moment. "I just wanted to say thanks, man. I'm breaking out onto the jam scene here in Nashville and you've opened a lot of doors for me." Chad said to him. Trey seemed honestly humbled and touched. I was impressed that Chad handled the situation so well.

If we had been having sex, we would have had very good sex that night.

The next day Chase emailed me. I sat and looked at his name on the screen for a few moments before opening the message. What would he have to say? How would it make me feel? I didn't want to have "Chase days" like I used to. I was really happy with Chad. That was where I wanted to be. I braced myself and I read.

Jan 19, 2005
I just wanted to say I'm sorry for blowing you off. You deserve better than me and I hope you've found it. I made the mistake of getting back together with Jana, who ended up cheating on me with some guy that has a stuttering problem. How's your perfect life? How's the man of your dreams? I'm sorry, I'm not meaning to be so bitter, it's just coming out that way and I know that everything I don't like in my own life is all my own fault. Anyway, I'm sorry and I hope you can forgive me someday.
Thanks for reading.
Chase

NINE – AN ATTAINABLE FUTURE

I was sorry that he was unhappy, but I wasn't sorry that I was happy. I had tried so hard but I couldn't give him whatever it was that he needed. I couldn't save him from himself. I wanted to write back, to give him a nod of thanks for offering an apology but not to offer friendship. As much as I wanted him to be in my life, I knew it would be dangerous. Feeling angry with him was a kind of protection and now his apology was taking that away from me. I didn't want to put myself into a situation where feelings for him could flood back into my heart. I found someone I loved.

Chad had something to offer me. He and I had a future. This was a relationship based not only on feelings or compatibility of interests but on the intersecting of our visions for our lives. I had grown up and I needed something different out of love than I had before.

Chad had started tanning and he'd gained a bit of muscle weight. He grew his facial hair from the bird-shaped goatee into a full, neatly trimmed beard, which I had my fingers in every chance I got. Oh, I loved that beard. I loved kissing him. I loved looking at him. I loved him.

Still, we had not said "I love you," and I wasn't sure why. It was obvious that we both felt it, and he had made references to it several times. I sure as heck wasn't going to say it first. We had one moment when we were lying together, looking into each other's eyes, and he said, "You're so in love." I had no witty retort; he was absolutely right, but he had the same look in his eyes. "You're in love too." He turned red as a rose.

While all this being in love was going on, Sophie's most recent boyfriend had cheated on her and they broke up. She'd been through quite a lot since I met Chad. One guy broke up with her because Jesus told him to, and then this one cheated on her. It was hard for me to watch her be so beaten down by love when it was lifting me to new heights, but we all get our turns, don't we?

March, 2005.

Two of my acquaintances were getting married on the same Saturday. It was odd enough that both weddings were the same day, but it was even odder that both couples invited me despite us only being acquaintances. One of the guys from my Belmont West group was marrying his high school sweetheart, and one of Lacey's friends was marrying her new love.

I put on a black Betsey dress and a blue shawl and curled my hair. Chad picked me up in the family BMW convertible. The first stop was Lacey's friend's reception, which was downtown in the building where my new church met. The ambiance was romantic, a very dim room with lots of candles. We danced, first to "At Last," and then to any other slow song they played, my head on his chest. I loved his height next to me; his solidity made me feel so secure. He had nicknamed me "tiny peanut" because I was always curled up next to him, so small.

Then, we were off to the dessert reception at a hotel. We danced some more as if we were the only people in the room. Everyone else could look at the bride and groom; we didn't need their eyes on us.

The night had gotten colder and I shivered in the car. Finally, wrapped up in warm covers in my bed, I drifted off to sleep—a tiny peanut next to the man she loved.

"Hey," Chad whispered. I barely heard him and I was awake only enough to make a small acknowledging sound.

"I love you."

"What did you say?" I asked. I was awake now. I turned to him and could see his eyes sparkle.

"I love you," he said again.

"I love you too!" I replied, relieved.

The floodgates had opened. Now that we could say it, we did—all the time. And we felt it too. Every day was a celebration that we had found each other.

He took me to a Titans game where I cheered for them but let it be known that I was a Steelers fan first. We drove to Pittsburgh where he met more of my friends and family and we saw *Dave Matthews Band* play. We had dinner at his parents' house once a week and would play scrabble with his brother. We went out with his friends to their favorite sports bar and with my friends to a local Steelers bar, and both groups of friends for two-for-one pizzas on Tuesdays.

He cooked for me or sometimes for his whole family. He made bacon wrapped scallops or pork tenderloin with some kind of secret sauce that tasted like heaven. We watched *Extreme Home Makeover* every Sunday and made tortellini for dinner together.

In addition to the beard and the tan, Chad had traded in his oval wire frames for chic brown glasses. Over time and with my encouragement he bought a new wardrobe and his clothes fit his tall muscular body properly now, unlike the baggy Old Navy jeans and oversized fleece he wore the first time he came to my apartment. He was becoming more and more handsome all the time.

The only downside to his new appearance was that the girls he had grown up with and had known all his life were starting to notice him in a different way. He told me about a girl who kept asking him to come over for a drink when her roommate was out. He kept telling her no. His band started playing other venues and the area in front of the stage would always be full of screaming girls. Most of the time I would sit back and laugh, but every now and then he would do something like take a cigarette from a girl and smoke it for a few minutes. I didn't know if it bothered me more that he was responding to the girl or because it wasn't his style to smoke.

One day after lunch, Chad and I stopped by a jewelry store known for carrying ornate, vintage-style designs. We were just going to look, but the salesman encouraged me to try one on. I didn't want to take it off, but I knew we weren't quite ready for that yet. We were in love, but we weren't going to rush things. We were in awe of each other and we weren't afraid.

June, 2005.

Chad graduated from college and took a job in car sales to support himself and his music career with the possibility of a master's degree as Plan B. I took a job in Tour Marketing and Promotions. I missed fashion, but I was getting my foot in the door in the music industry and I was one step closer to my dream of helping artists shape their careers. I really liked the job, the artists that I worked with and my coworkers. Things were moving forward at a good pace-one step at a time.

I got another random email from Chase that he titled "Mr. Brightside," in which he talked about a band called *The Killers*, his plans to stay with his brother for a while, and nothing else in particular. I didn't really have anything to say back so again I didn't respond.

I kept in touch with one of my clients from Betsey Johnson, who was a real estate agent and who told me about the growing condo market in Nashville. It would be smart to invest in something now as the market grows, I realized. Chad was excited, too, so the agent took us to see some of the condos. We loved the style and location of one near Music Row, and my parents lent me the money for a down payment. The condo was in my name alone, which I thought was a good thing to do until we were married. It would be my home first, then our first home.

Chad and I were sharing our lives. I could see it like the steel beams that were going up to frame our building. I could practically hold it in my hands like the contract on which I had signed my name, where we wrote in our choices for granite and flooring. We didn't just have dreams, we had an attainable future.

He Was Trying

In between the moon and you
The angels get a better view
Of the crumbling difference
Between wrong and right
Counting Crows

August 16, 2005.

It was a normal Wednesday morning at the office. I was talking with some radio folks about the tours that I was promoting and sending posters and stickers out to country music bars. Early in the afternoon, Meredith messaged me online and asked if I was busy or if I was available to talk.

Though we regularly talked from our offices throughout the day, I knew something was different. I went out in the hall and sat on the tan leather couch. My heart started beating faster and my vision was a little blurred. My mind was spinning while I called her.

My first thought was that something had happened to my first boyfriend who spent most nights at the local bar and then drove himself home. However, when Meredith began to speak it wasn't his name she said.

"Chase died last night."

No!

No no no no no no no!

A million questions followed and Meredith didn't have many answers for me at that point. She knew it was a drug overdose but didn't know how or what. She knew his mom had been the one to find him. She didn't know whether it was suicide or accidental. She, of course, assured me she would do anything I needed and to please call her later.

I left work immediately and called Chad, Sophie, and my parents. I didn't cry until I left the office, at which point I sobbed violently all the way home to the apartment that I was now sharing with Sophie.

I got home before she did and crumbled to the floor. She found me an hour or so later, sitting in the laundry basket. I wasn't sure how I got in there but I realized then that

TEN – HE WAS TRYING

I'd been folding my underwear over and over again. There was now a neat stack of pastel cotton and lace next to the laundry basket. She helped me out, sat me on the bed, and let me talk and cry and talk and cry. We were both in disbelief. *How could this happen*, I kept thinking. *This can't be real. Can't I just wake him up and tell him how much we all love him and we don't want him to go?*

On the phone earlier, Chad told me that he had some things to do and he would be over later. I was hurt by his obvious failure to be there in a time when I needed him badly, but I considered the possibility that he didn't understand what a big deal this was. He knew who Chase was, but rarely did I mention Chase to Chad. He did come over that night and sleep in the bed with me. He held me while I cried, a kind of crying I never wanted to experience again. It felt like a dark hopelessness had taken over me. It felt like someone had turned out the lights in my heart.

The darkness that I felt was palpable. I didn't sleep for days. I dreaded bedtime because that was when I was alone with my thoughts and when the awareness that he was gone, really, forever gone, became acute and unavoidable.

I did find out that Chase's death was an accident. He had been on Methadone, a drug designed to curb the urges of heroin addicts, only that it is lethal when mixed with heroin. Chase gave in, just one time, and it killed him.

I went back to the email he had sent me just the week before. Was he reaching out to me? I hadn't answered him yet and now I never could.

```
August 10, 2005 "He was trying"
Everything has turned to shit, to be honest. I am seeing someone and she is very sweet and laughs at everything I say and she thinks I'm cute, so that's good. Other than that I've been struggling with addiction. I won't say to what, so you won't think I'm shit, but I ended up going to rehab for a month and am fighting urges, and sometimes losing to them every day. I go to meetings and have a sponsor. The light at the end of the tunnel, though, is if I can get 6 months clean (God willing) I will be able to go back to school, which is what I really want to do. How are you? I'm sure you're doing fabulous and I hope you are happy nowadays.
Take pains, be perfect.
Chase
```

TEN – HE WAS TRYING

I couldn't get off work to go to the funeral. If I had insisted on going, I'm sure my boss wouldn't have fired me but I knew that at the funeral I would be there with a crowd of people who were sad that Chase was gone but never truly knew him. I wanted more than that. I knew him better than anyone. I wanted to be with the family, not the crowd, so I decided not to fight my boss about it. Instead, I planned to go up there on his birthday to spend that time alone with his mom, and to grieve the way I needed to grieve.

Didn't he know how important he was? I could not come to terms with the fact that I would never again talk to him. He would never make me laugh again. He would never introduce me to a new band that would take my life in a different direction and he would never hold my hand or stare into my eyes with his bigger blue eyes. One little slip—a mistake! My heart was absolutely broken.

I spent some time staring at the picture in which we looked so alike, thinking about how similar we really were. We were both ruled by passion and creativity—only his was met with desperation and mine with caution. His darkness tried to claw its way out while I had to purposely stir mine. I decided I didn't believe in soul mates. If there was such a thing, I wanted to believe he was mine, but where did that leave Chad? It wasn't fair so I rejected the concept.

October, 2005.

When I went to see Chase's mom, she cried a lot while I cried a little. The house looked and smelled just as I remembered it and I could not believe Chase wasn't waiting in his room for me to come in. I told his mom this. She got up and walked to the mantle and asked if I wanted to hold him, then she handed me a very pretty urn.

She told me how much Chase loved me, how she knew that he and I were meant to be together, but she was happy for me that I was doing well in Nashville and that I had found someone special. I promised her that I would help her to keep his memory alive, and that I would never forget him, not a single thing about him.

I didn't ask to go into his room that day. I couldn't bear it.

On the drive home, I tried so hard to imagine him in the passenger seat next to me. I thought that if I could remember the details clearly enough or beg God or Chase's soul or whatever convincingly enough, that just for a moment he would truly be sitting there beside me. However, that's not how it works. I was left here, in this world, to drive on alone.

He was sixteen when I met him and he was twenty-one when he died. Roughly sixty-three months I knew him.

TEN – HE WAS TRYING

Some months he commanded and others we didn't even speak at all. Sixty-three months is something I could map. I could see it. I could take it apart and put it back together like an engine, studying it inside and out. But I couldn't pinpoint a singular source; the impact that those sixty-three months would have on the rest of my unfinished life would always seem mysteriously huge.

Every day got a little easier. They say grief is only relieved by the replacement of the thing that's been lost or if the griever adjusts permanently to accommodate the loss. Chase could not be replaced, though that's not to say I couldn't be truly happy and in love with someone else. I suppose I did begin to adjust to the loss the longer I lived with it. That's how it felt—that the loss of him had a life of its own. I lived with it as I could have lived with him. Some nights it was quiet and sometimes it pounded on my door. Some days we would argue and some nights we would dance.

There would never come a day that I wouldn't miss Chase. I promised to myself that I would always believe in an alternate universe in which we lived our artist life in our little apartment in the city, where nothing else mattered except that we were there together.

11
A Devil Named Denial

November 2005.

Chad and I were talking more seriously about marriage. He emailed me pictures of rings while I was at work, filling my head with daydreams and making it hard to focus. I would rather be on wedding websites, getting ideas for flowers, dresses and cakes, than calling two-step bars in Tucson asking if they wanted some Reba McEntire posters.

He started asking me if I would marry him much like he had told me he loved me—first out of the blue, then constantly. We'd be lying in bed in the apartment that he now lived in with his band's drummer and he'd ask, "Will you marry me?" While the Mythbusters blew something up on TV, he'd ask "Will you marry me?" Driving to meet friends at a restaurant, he'd ask, "Will you marry me?" I said yes every time. He even began to refer to me as his fiancée.

My life was unfolding in front of me—a straight and narrow path. This was what being grown up was like. This was real life; things had turned out all right after all.

My parents came to town to spend Thanksgiving with Chad's family. It was the first time our parents would meet. It was a very big deal. Chad and I had been together for over a year and it was obvious that things were serious.

Thanksgiving morning, Chad called.

"My mom isn't feeling well. Would you and your family mind fending for yourselves today? I'm so sorry…"

"No!" I insisted. "It's Thanksgiving, we haven't prepared, we can't get food now! What's going on?"

Chad admitted that his mom was having a breakdown and had locked herself in the bathroom. I had learned over the past year that this is something she did from time to time. *But not today!*

"Ok, I'll take care of it," he said.

When we arrived, the house looked and smelled beautiful and his mom was smiling. I was going to have to deal with this forever, I thought, but Chad was worth it and I was sure that as far as in-laws went, it could have been much worse.

Chad was barely present. He hardly paid attention to the conversation if he was even in the room at all. I wondered if his mother had done something to upset him.

We were sound asleep in his bed the next week when his phone rang. "No, I'm sleeping. I'm not coming out tonight," he told someone. Then he hung up the phone. "That was my friend Jordan. She always wants me to come out late at night," he said. He held me tighter and fell back asleep while I wondered why I had never met Jordan and why he didn't say, "I'm in bed with my girlfriend/fiancée/future wife."

December 2005.

I spent Christmas in Pittsburgh. Chad's family was sad that I wouldn't be able to be with them on Christmas so we had our own holiday celebration before I left. His mom had asked for a list of things that I wanted and I gave her a few ideas. She bought me all of them, which was nice and completely unexpected. I think she was overcompensating, but still, I was very touched. After I opened a new purse, a book, my favorite hair product and a bottle of perfume, Chad announced that he had to run off to an emergency band practice.

ELEVEN – A DEVIL NAMED DENIAL

"It's my Christmas with your family," I protested.

"I know, Peanut, but the guys really need me and they're already mad that I haven't been around much."

My fault, of course.

"Well, I'd like to stay and visit with your family then," I said. I was being the good wife.

He went. I couldn't believe it.

A few nights later some friends of mine were having a Christmas party. Chad had plans with the guys and couldn't come. We usually made it a point to plan guy's nights and girl's nights but not when one of us had something like this going on—an event that we should attend together. Half-heartedly apologetic, he said that he would call me when he could get away. Sophie and I went to the party together. I wore a festive burnt-orange and gold sweater with a falsely pleasant expression.

The more time that passed without Chad calling, the more wine I drank. I talked with Lacey, with one of the guys from work and with some of the girls. I laughed and posed for pictures. Then I had more wine. I saw some of Ethan's friends arrive so I texted him to see if he was coming too. He hadn't been planning on it, but he said he would come by.

I wandered in a wine fog to the little bathroom to pee and selected a Chanel perfume bottle from the shelf in the bathroom. I over-sprayed myself, as my sense of smell had been too dull to tell how much I had on.

Ethan arrived and I stood near to him, clutching my wine, asking about his life and going on and on about my cool music business job, my absent fiancée and my condo that was under construction. My hands moved dramatically as I talked and I spilled some wine on my sweater. I brushed at it and kept talking and smiling.

Suddenly, Chad was there. I hadn't seen him come in.

"Hello," he said, suspiciously.

"Oh!" I gulped. "Ethan, this is my boyfriend, Chad!" Chad said hello and excused us. He pulled me away to where we could have our own conversation.

"I came to take you home," he said.

"I'm not ready to leave yet!" I slurred. "And you're supposed to be here to hang out with my friends too."

"You're very drunk and I'm tired," he said. "We need to go home."

We argued for a few more minutes before I gave a few sloppy goodbye hugs and pouted my way out the door.

Once he had buckled my seatbelt, I set about the task of convincing him that I wasn't drunk. I could hear my words slurring but I wouldn't give up.

"Who was that guy?" Chad asked.

ELEVEN – A DEVIL NAMED DENIAL

"Who? Oh, Ethan. An old friend from college," I said casually.

"Did you date him?"

"No, just a friend," I lied.

During the few minutes of silence that followed, I passed out. Chad helped me walk to his apartment and settled me in bed.

"Where did you get that perfume?" he asked when he climbed in the bed next to me.

"Ummm, the ba...bathroom at the party," I replied.

"Don't ever wear it again," he said bluntly. He had been angry with me already, but wasn't it his fault for not being there with me?

"Why?" I whispered, glad that sleep would be an escape from the icy chill in his voice.

"My ex wore it," he said.

"Oh. I'm sorry," I said. "I'm really sorry."

I wanted him to hold me. I wanted him not to be mad at me anymore. What would I do if I lost him? I needed him not to be mad at me. He held me, but even in my sleep I knew that something was off. I thought it was my fault.

The next day, on a dreary December Sunday morning, we had sex. It was so strange how it happened. We had waited over a year then suddenly, both sober and feeling sorry, we made the choice to go there.

We looked into each other's eyes. It was quiet, unlike our playful kissing and messing around. This was a band-aid, trying to fix a problem that I didn't even recognize but was covering up. Afterward, we lay still and repeated over and over how we loved each other so very much—each making sure that the other was convinced that things were still the same.

But things weren't the same. There was a little devil on my shoulder named Denial and I gave him all my attention, absentmindedly flicking away his friend called Wake-Up-and-Smell-the-End.

Sophie and I decided to host a New Year's party. I had the perfect fuchsia and purple dress from Betsey Johnson. I had worn it on Valentine's Day earlier that year when Chad brought me flowers and took me to Virago for dinner. That was when things were perfect.

New Year's Eve day I was preparing the food and confirming the details with some guests, many of whom were stopping by our place first before going to other parties. Chad called to announce that his roommate decided to throw a party too, and he had to stay there to protect his stuff. The

ELEVEN – A DEVIL NAMED DENIAL

last time that they had thrown a party someone peed in his room and he feared for the safety of his musical equipment.

"Just lock your door!" I told him. If he really wanted to be at my party, he could be.

"It's more than that," he said. "Most of the stuff in this apartment is mine and these people get out of control."

"Fine," I said. "My party ends early anyway so why don't you just stop by here towards the end of mine and then I'll come with you to yours."

He agreed.

By the time Chad got to my place, everyone had left for the other parties and he was blasted drunk. Knowing that I had a right to be upset with him, he walked away from our conversation and went into the kitchen. I heard him make a drink and then slide down the wall and land on the kitchen floor with a thump.

"Chad. Get up," I said, walking into the kitchen and tugging on his limp arm. I could hear the countdown start on the TV.

Ten. Nine.

He looked up at me with a mischievous smile.

"I love you," he said, getting up on one knee. "Will you marry me, peanut?

Six. Five.

"Yes, yes," I answered. "I will. I'm upset with you but I'm still going to marry you!"

Two. One.

He downed half his drink in one swallow.

Happy New Year!

The night only got worse. I changed into jeans and drove us back to his apartment where there was a raging party. Someone was throwing up in the bathroom and people were sitting on the kitchen counters yelling at other people in the same room. It was too loud for my sober mood.

I said hello to some of Chad's friends who had become my friends too, many of whom hugged me and wished me a happy new year. I was surprised by how many people that I didn't know. When did he start hanging out with new people?

I snapped some pictures of Chad and his friends whether I knew them or not and posed for a couple of shots with his band mates and some of the girls. One girl that I didn't know who was pretty and thin with curly red hair took a picture with me. I think maybe I'd seen her at some of their shows but I couldn't tell who she was there with.

Suddenly Chad was in the mood to pay attention to me. He dragged me by the hand to his room and kissed me. I liked when his mouth tasted of alcohol, usually, but this was different. I could have lit his breath on fire. He tried to push

ELEVEN – A DEVIL NAMED DENIAL

me against the wall, playfully, but he pushed me so hard that I spun around and hit the wall face first.

I heard my nose crack and it started gushing blood. Chad was surprised and immediately remorseful. He ran to get me some tissue from the bathroom across the hall. I sat on the bed and held the tissue to my nose. It hurt but it wasn't broken.

"I'm so sorry, baby," Chad said, trying to hug me. I knew he was sincere but I pushed him away.

"Don't touch me!" I cried, still in shock. *What is happening to us*, I wondered. Each incident alone was nothing to be concerned about but the off nights just kept piling up.

I was too embarrassed to go back to the party so I changed into a t-shirt and boxers from my drawer of stuff and got in bed. Chad went to say goodnight to a few people and came to bed too. I was fine by then and I wasn't angry; I knew it was an accident. So I let him hold me.

"I'm sorry. I'm so sorry," he said over and over.

12
How to Be Single

January, 2006.

The first week of the New Year, Chad had daily band practices in order to get ready for a show where they were going to debut a lot of new material.

"I think this will be good for us to have a little time apart," he said. "I'll miss you, though."

I thought it was strange; the week was long and uncomfortable. Usually, we stayed the night together or at the very least, we were each other's first and last call of the day. However, during that week, he didn't call much, blaming long practices and too much time spent trying to get some of his equipment fixed. He kept reminding me that it was good for us to have space.

TWELVE – HOW TO BE SINGLE

I didn't want space. I wanted to know why this was happening. Then, I got my wish and I wanted to take it back.

The day before the show, Chad asked me to stop by his apartment. I sat on the living room floor with him, so glad to see him after our first ever week apart, but he never took his eyes of the guitar that he was re-stringing.

That's when I first saw what was coming, why he'd asked me to come over.

"I think we should take a break," he said. "I've just been feeling a lot of pressure saving money for a ring and talking about getting married and I'm not sure that I'm ready for all of that." He said that he needed to sort some things out for himself before he could imagine being married. Was it time for him to give up the dream of being a musician? What was he doing with his life?

On that one, I agreed. What *was* he doing with his life? And why did he have to make these decisions without me? Wasn't the point of building a life together exactly that? *Our* life together? I was the opposite of the people in *The Quarterlife Crisis* book, and here I was in love with a guy who was having a quarter-life crisis. I couldn't understand what was wrong with him; he was the one who was always talking about getting married!

I felt stupid to have believed this would be effortless. I felt scared that a break was really the end. I felt angry that he was hurting me and that he didn't believe in us like I did. I decided that I would have to have enough faith for the both of us. Then, I went numb. I turned my heart off and switched on the autopilot.

"Okay," I said. "Do what you need to do I guess. Just, call me when you want. I won't call you. You're the one who wants space."

I put my coat on, walked to my car, turned the key, and drove home. I walked to my door, went inside and lay down on my bed.

Then, I fell apart.

At first I thought I was going to die. My heart was beating so fast for days that I thought finally it might explode. I threw up what little food I ate. I cried and I didn't sleep. I called off work and then called Chad to officially break up with him. I just couldn't take the waiting. I thought it was inevitable and I wanted to get it over with. He assured me that the break was just that—a break—so I agreed to wait it out. However, I needed some parameters. If I couldn't understand why this change was necessary, at least I could have some control over the guidelines of our new arrange-

TWELVE – HOW TO BE SINGLE

ment. We were still together; we would call each other and could still say "I love you," but we wouldn't hang out much.

Everyone seemed to think this was about Chad having cold feet. "Men have trouble making big decisions when they are based on emotion. He'll come around," Dad said. The Jamison's had been through a time apart before they were married, Mrs. Jamison told me. This is normal.

I prayed a lot. I didn't want to be with Chad if that was truly not what God wanted for me but then why did I feel so much love for him?

"You can rejoice in that love," my pastor told me. "God blessed you with being able to feel that way about someone, whether or not the feelings are returned."

Wait, the feelings aren't returned?

I read an article in *Elle Magazine* called "How to be Single," in which the writer declared that Lean Cuisine and *Law and Order* reruns are better than dying. *I do love Law and Order*, I thought. The article got me thinking about what I could do during the break that would help me grow. I could get back into yoga, painting and writing. Somehow, with Chad, I never got to do any of those things. All I had been doing was playing wife. I decided I would fill the emptiness in me with God and with paint.

Some days, Chad would call and say he wanted me back. I'd tell him that I had to think about it. I was guarding my heart now that I knew what kind of damage he could do to it. I didn't trust him. Some days, he'd call and say he still didn't know what he wanted. I told him that he had to want to be with me so badly that he couldn't stand it or I wasn't interested.

I had told him that I wasn't going to call him; he would have to contact me. He wanted space and I was going to give it to him. He wouldn't hear from me at all. But I was so sick. I wasn't eating, sleeping or getting any work done. Even worse, I was waking up with heart palpitations and nausea every morning, choking into the toilet at 6:00 a.m. and then crying in bed until I absolutely had to get up for work. My first conscious thought every morning was that something was terribly wrong. And it was.

Chad never left me alone for long. A few days would go by and he would text me, "You're still my tiny peanut," or send me a picture of our partially constructed condo with the caption "home." I would become so excited that he still loved me and still thought that I was his future, and then I wouldn't hear anything for days.

Eventually, he told me he had met someone. He didn't expect it, he said. "It wasn't a big deal," he was just taking advantage of the opportunity to see someone else so that he

TWELVE – HOW TO BE SINGLE

could be sure that I was the one. He was seeing someone else. To be more sure. That I was the one.

I knew it wasn't right, but I had committed myself to this man and I didn't know how to detach myself. I was trying to be sympathetic, understanding and courageous but I was sympathetic, understanding and courageous with our best interest in mind. Not my own. I couldn't bear to think of myself that way. One single person. Without him.

So I waited.

I wrote to myself as if I was writing to Chad.

```
I wish I could call you. You would sleep-
ily say "Heeeey," and I'd say, "Hi," and
you'd say "What's wrong?" "I can't
sleep." I woke up and I can't stop think-
ing about you and my heart's pounding too
fast for me to fall back asleep. It's
like...You know how I tell you that you
make my heart swell? Well, without you
it's too tiny and has to work extra hard
to pump blood through my body. It's been
hammering away for an hour, and I feel so
cold. I can't stop shaking.
```

I listened to Lori McKenna. "Well I never told you to love me, that's your sort of greed." I listened to Patty Griffin. "Let's take a walk on the bridge, right over this mess." I listened to everyone tell me it would be all right and I pretended to believe them. I listened to everyone but myself.

In the past, knowing that Chase was still out there would have been a comfort to me. Maybe our paths would cross again. Maybe we were meant to be together and had just been apart for a while—for some greater purpose. But Chase wasn't there anymore and the *what-ifs* began pouring in. What if I had fought harder for Chase when I had the chance? Would he still be here? Would we be together and happy and I wouldn't be hurting and broken and sick and he wouldn't be gone? If Chad wasn't the one and Chase was gone, what would become of me?

February, 2006.

Sophie, Lacey and I began planning weekly girls' nights. Sometimes it was hard for me to do anything but focus on holding back my tears for one evening, but on other nights the girls really helped me escape from my nightmare.

One night, while on my way, Lacey called me from where we were supposed to be meeting.

TWELVE – HOW TO BE SINGLE

"Kim, I went in to the sushi place next door to use the bathroom and Chad is there. I just wanted you to know."

I had always hated their sushi.

"Well, I'm a block away so I'm coming," I said. "I doubt they'll come over to the bar."

"Okay," Lacey replied.

When it came to break-ups, I generally thought ignorance was bliss, especially with how sick this was making me. I made it a life-saving point not to look on his Myspace page for fear of what I might or might not find. I didn't want to know her name or anything about her. However, on this particular night, I had a moment of weakness.

Lacey told me that they were visible through the window of the restaurant. She said that if I was absolutely sure that I wanted to see them, she would walk with me and show me where they were sitting. We walked towards the restaurant and then I stopped short. I stood there for a moment looking at the street. He didn't love me anymore. He was on a date with another girl. He wasn't mine. I wasn't his. The thoughts were so strange. I knew that I needed to see it to believe it.

"Okay, where?" I asked, turning towards the window.

They were at the sushi bar and I could see the back of their heads. I saw his dark hair covered by a brown ball cap. I saw that he was wearing a shirt that I bought him.

I saw her curly red ponytail.

I swear it was the train that kept me alive those months. I would go to bed so early—beyond exhausted from working hard just to breathe in and out all day, from the effort that it took to get through one hour without dissolving into tears. I was in bed by eight o'clock, sometimes seven. I would lie in bed awake, feeling like I was on the ocean floor, waiting for sleep to wash over me like a wave. But the tide just wouldn't take me.

Alone in the silence, no longer having the distractions of work to do or the voices of loved ones on the phone pumping me with encouragement, I would be overtaken by hysteria and cry until I physically ached. Then, at 10:00pm, between whimpers, I would hear the train. In the cold darkness, my friend whistled, wanting so badly to be heard by anyone who would listen. The train was lonely too. I wasn't alone. Only then, each night, did a wave of relief wash over me, bringing sleep at last.

Still, come morning, my eyes would fly open at dawn, hot tears pouring from them. My heart would race faster than I believed was possible and the adrenaline would make me nauseous. Over and over again. I couldn't understand how my heart could beat so fast if I was lying completely still and if I had been asleep just moments before. It was as if I

TWELVE – HOW TO BE SINGLE

was running from the hurt in my dreams. Trying to control my heart, I concentrated on each breath. In slowly. Out slowly. Still, I felt so sick that I would rush to the bathroom and dry heave into the toilet, saliva and tears falling into the waiting water. I never could get anything to come out of my empty stomach, as I was only able to eat every three days or so.

Sophie, precious Sophie, never once made me feel at fault for being so sick. It had to be horrible for her to wake up every day to the sound of me in the bathroom. I felt so guilty that I never purposely woke her to talk or ask her to sit with me. I gave her as much silence and space as I could manage. If my distance would keep her kind, I would give her that.

It was hard for me too, being able to see in her eyes that she didn't recognize me. I didn't recognize myself either, and that was difficult enough to bear. It wasn't that loving Chad had changed me, it was losing him, and it changed me so completely that it was as if my entire DNA had been reconstructed.

March, 2006.

Finally, I went to a doctor. Emotionally, I had good days and bad days, but physically I was so ill that I was rapidly losing weight, unable to eat or sleep and still having panic attacks in the morning.

"My boyfriend and I broke up or are on a break or something, so I thought I was just upset about that, but it's been two months," I told the doctor.

The doctor ran heart tests, blood tests and asked me all kinds of questions about my many symptoms. I went from just being below my highest weight ever, 140 pounds, to less than 120 pounds in two months. It wasn't that I was choosing not to eat, rather, it was that I was either flat out not hungry or I would be so sick in the mornings that anything I had eaten came back up. I was rail thin. Sophie called me a bobble-head because my head looked too big for my skin-and-bones body.

The doctor called with the results. I had hyperthyroidism, he said, which accounted for the anxiety attacks, low appetite and high metabolism. He explained that my thyroid regulated all of these things and its over-activity from stress had me all out of whack. Instead of putting me on a medication to regulate the thyroid itself, the doctor put me on anti-anxiety medication. "Hyperthyroidism is common among divorced women," he told me. "This kind of severe emotional stress can cause the thyroid to overwork." If my anxiety levels are regulated, he said, my thyroid should fix itself.

TWELVE – HOW TO BE SINGLE

The *Lexapro* would take two weeks to work into my system, but little by little I started to function like a regular member of society again.

Still, work was too much for me to handle. I couldn't focus. I needed a change of environment where I wasn't in a still, dim office all day, and where I could be around more people and be under less pressure. So I left a job that I loved and went back to work in retail.

Chad was destroying me in every way possible.

April, 2006.
Chad was still hot and cold, telling me that I would be his wife one day or that he was "almost" ready to get back together, and then acting like I had made it up the next day. He was a stranger to me on the phone. We hadn't even seen each other in person in months.

Some nights he would tell me that he might stop by and surprise me. I would sit up waiting, listening to every creek in the screen door, but there was never a knock.

I made friends at the boutique where I was working and I would sometimes go out with them dancing or to local fashion shows. I excelled in sales, and despite my daily crying sessions in the stock room, my boss, Taryn, was patient with me.

One of my customers was a guy who worked for Sony Records. He would come in to bring us CDs to play in the store and we would always end up chatting about music. His name was Ben Moren. I was surprised to learn that he was a year younger; he gave off an air of mature confidence. Ben was short and fair with dirty blonde hair and beard, and freckled arms. One day he brought me a copy of a live *Counting Crows* CD that I didn't have yet. I must have mentioned that they were my favorite band. I gave him my phone number even though I knew I wasn't ready.

Chad was still seeing the girl. That's what I called her, *the girl*. Dripping with disgust, to him, to my parents and to my friends, I would call her, *the girl*. One day, she wandered into the store, probably by mistake, and I had to excuse myself to the back room. She must have seen me because it wasn't long before she left. Chad told me once that she was afraid of me because she knew how much he loved me. He told me that we were actually very much alike. I liked that she was afraid. I refused to believe that we were alike.

One night I was out for pizza with a friend, waiting for a table. Chad and *the girl* walked in and spotted me, looking suddenly unsure of their next move. It was too late for us to ignore each other. Chad shook his head and said, "I'm sorry, we'll leave." I was too upset to stay so my friend and I left also. I was driving home when Chad called.

I answered.

"I'm so sorry about that! Listen, she's crazy and jealous and she told me she never wanted to fucking see me again and I'm relieved. I'm going back to meet up with some friends. Will you come? It's over with her and I want you. She's so crazy."

I went. We kissed and laughed, and there was magic in the air. This is what I had been waiting for. Even his friends kept telling me how glad they were that we were back together; they didn't like her much at all. Knowing that I didn't want to know her name, they used a code name, Jay, whenever they talked about her.

The next morning, Chad and I were on the phone talking sweetly to each other when there was a knock at the door. I had on a t-shirt with a hole in the armpit. I hadn't brushed my teeth or put in my contacts but there he was and it was exactly like I'd hoped. He took me to lunch and he kissed me goodbye. He said that he felt like he was coming home.

Then things went right back to the way they were, hot and cold. Four calls in one day then four days without a call. A week went by, then two.

I took myself to a museum to see an exhibit of French impressionist paintings: Van Gogh, Renoir and Monet. My favorites were a LaTour and one called "Wildflowers" by Redon. I went to the movies, where I ate peanut M&Ms and checked my phone a few times even though I'd promised myself I'd turn it off. I watched *Law and Order.* I wrote—wrote all the things that I couldn't say to him. I wrote about how much I believed in us. I wrote about how much I trusted God. I wrote that I was praying for him. I wrote down all the jokes that I could remember, which weren't many.

I met a guy at work who was very attractive and my type: tall, dark-haired, stylish and most likely a musician. He had fingernails painted black and he kept smiling at me. He exuded confidence in the way he slipped into different jackets and checked himself out in the mirror. The way he tried on a hat, I could tell he didn't need me to tell him that it looked great on him. He wasn't cocky, just confident. He asked me to put the hat on hold and told me that his name was Quinn. It was so good that I had to repeat it. He turned to ask me my name before walking out the door.

I wrote my phone number on the hold tag with the hat. He had mentioned that he was from Vancouver so I knew that while proving to myself that I wasn't living for Chad anymore, I was still safe from stepping into a situation

TWELVE – HOW TO BE SINGLE

that would require me to move on. There was no way I would actually begin to date Quinn.

I loved the idea of this guy, though. We would have long talks on the phone about cities that he had visited, and we would be very open and very deep, sharing with each other our passions and our dreams. Perhaps he would write me song lyrics and email them to me. We'd get trapped in each other's minds. Chad and I would get trapped in one of our apartments together, but we were never in each other's minds that way.

Is that really true? I wondered after the new thought crossed my mind. Were we not perfect for each other after all?

Was I starting to let go?

May, 2006.

I began dreaming of fighting with Chad every night, and the dreams began to include other girls. My nights were filled with hatred. My days were heavy with his phone calls, or the lack of phone calls—heavy either way. I was a yo-yo, just a little toy in his hands. I never knew anyone could make me hurt that much, but I didn't know what to do about it. If I was to walk away, then I surely wouldn't have him and wasn't that worse?

I lay in bed practicing my "I can't do this anymore" speech for several weeks before one night something clicked. I realized that I had gotten it right and I was going to have to use it. I sobbed. I prayed, "Please, God, no. Tell me I don't have to do this!" but all I felt was confirmation.

I told Chad that I couldn't wait any longer. I had been his girlfriend in my heart for four months, and he hadn't been my boyfriend in his heart. I was much more invested than he was and the inconsistencies were too hard on me.

He said, "You're right, it isn't fair to you," and we got off the phone.

I couldn't believe it was that easy for him, but I felt a kind of bittersweet relief. Then, a few hours later, he texted me and accused me of seeing someone else.

Maybe I wasn't the yo-yo.

He would text me and I would ignore him. He sent videos of himself playing guitar. He sent "I love you so much" messages—anything to get me to finally answer him. Then, he'd say triumphantly, "you replied!" It was a game to him. I reminded him that "anything shy of being my boyfriend wasn't enough for me."

"I need a yes or no," I said, "and I need it yesterday." I went on trying to ignore him.

TWELVE – HOW TO BE SINGLE

It got worse. The last week of May, Chad was still flirting with me by text on Sunday. Monday, he said he still loved me to which I didn't reply. Wednesday, he got a girlfriend. Thursday, I found out and all hell broke loose. I was so confused. I fought for this relationship so hard, but the person he had become was not someone I wanted to be with. I knew that person could never be my boyfriend, my husband or *the one*. It was time to let go.

I wasn't surprised when I heard that he had started dating *the girl* again, even though he'd said she was crazy. *I'll show you crazy*, I thought. I drove over to his apartment late at night in a raging thunderstorm and pounded on his window until he came to the door. When he stepped out and stood in the rain instead of inviting me in, I knew she was in there. The girl. "Jay."

The red ponytail had taken my place.

"You like her more than me." I said to myself more than to him.

"I can't compare. This is just what I need right now. My family likes her, and..."

I interrupted, "I need you to say it to me. Tell me you like her more than me."

"But I..."

"Say it!"

"I like her more than you."

"Do not ever call me again," I whispered. "Not. Ever!"

I didn't wait for a response; I had heard everything I needed to hear.

I was dripping with rain and ecstatic with relief. I still needed to heal but at least that process could finally begin.

13
Objects in Mirror

July, 2006.

That summer, I was coming out of the gloom of my anxiety and heartbreak but was still a walking open wound. Now that Chad wasn't in my daily life and I was supposed to be "moving on," it was no longer acceptable for me to excuse myself from the sales floor at work to cry or talk to friends for hours about myself, my feelings and my theories. So I pretended that I was moving on; maybe if I pretended hard enough, it would happen. At the very least, pretending would help me hold on to my friends and prevent me from being locked in the psych ward.

Pretending was easy when I wasn't coherent. I would go out with my work friends and drink until I blacked out, baffled at how I got home safely every time. I would sleep it off, get up in the morning and smile through another day.

I am ready, I am fine. I am fine.

I was still too thin from having been so sick, but now I could wear flat boots with shorts and silk racerback tanks that were just a little too loose for me. I thought that I looked like a 60's icon. I would dance until three a.m. and I wouldn't wash off my makeup. I would just add a little more to it the next morning. Yesterday's eyeliner always looks better, anyway.

Objects in mirror are more fucked up than they appear.

I met someone. Ok, truth be told, I met lots of someones. There was Sam, shockingly attractive, who stopped me one night outside *The Red Door*. I was leaving the bar unusually early, but he convinced me to come back in with him. It wasn't a hard sell—it was his birthday, after all. He was from Ohio and he was visiting some friends in town. I caught a glimpse of his ID as he ordered our *Yaegerbombs*. His birthday was actually in March but we celebrated anyway.

Then, there was that one guy from the dance party at Ombi Bar. I have a picture with him. Oh, what was his name? I think he had an accent. I don't even remember taking the picture, though my eyes are focused properly and I look completely lucid. It's a great skill to have—to take sober-looking pictures when you're anything but.

There was Vince, the drummer, who I met at a cook-out. He looked like he could have been Chase's brother. He was several years younger and still in college. We went out a few times; he even introduced me to his dad, which I thought was nice, but then I lost interest.

There was a little game that I played with the guys I met. In order to validate myself, I would do everything in my power to capture the attention of anyone who caught mine. We'd dance, kiss and maybe hang out once or twice. Then they would realize that we weren't suited for each other, which I knew deep down, and they'd stop calling. Despite the fact that I didn't have feelings for any of them, each rejection stung like a slap in the face.

On the off chance that someone stayed interested in me, I would back off—out of boredom, maybe. Out of fear, probably. It doesn't really matter why. None of them were right for me, and I wasn't right for any of them. They just made me feel less alone for a little while. Each guy stamped the passport of my heart. "You're worthy." Stamp, "You're enough." "You have not failed completely." Stamp, stamp.

Ben from Sony kept calling too. He was on the Warped Tour for the summer so we got to know each other better over the phone. I think the distance made me feel safe, and not being able to rush things kept me from ruining it. *Counting Crows* were coming to town in August and he bought us tickets. The man knew the way straight to my heart—my black and blue heart.

There was something different about him; maybe it was because he was only on the phone—therefore mysterious and less threatening—or maybe because he was so casual, friendly and seemingly normal. Most of the others were as dysfunctional as I was, and although Ben wasn't perfect, he had his head fixed firmly on his shoulders.

Ben returned from tour mid-July during a week that I was staying with the Jamison kids. He and I had built up a pretty significant amount of anticipation for getting to see each other so he came over to the house instead of waiting until I was done babysitting. He took us out for ice cream, then we all played cards. I was pleased that he just wanted to hang out and spend time getting to know me. It was already the healthiest relationship that I'd had in a long time.

The Jamison's returned while we were still playing cards. The sun was just sinking in the sky, casting a yellow-orange glow over the golf course behind the house. We left

THIRTEEN – OBJECTS IN MIRROR

and he followed me back to my apartment, where Sophie was watching some pop culture game show on TV. We sat and watched with her for a while. I could feel the tension of sitting next to someone new and the excitement building between us as each team's score rose higher on the show.

Finally, Sophie handed us the remote and went to bed. I changed the channel to something not embarrassing but only mildly interesting. While Ben told me stories from the tour, I could only think about how different he was, physically, from other guys that I usually went for. For one, he was barely taller than me, and I would surely be looking straight into his eyes when I wore heels. Nevertheless, his stride was so confident that he gave the appearance of being taller than he was. He also had fair hair and was freckled; he did have a beard though, scoring one point for my type. His eyes were small but were a surprisingly pretty gray-blue.

I was looking into his eyes as he talked, and suddenly I realized that he was holding my hand. When did that happen? How had I missed it? Did I mind? I decided that I didn't, and we traced our fingers over each others' palms as our quiet conversation continued. We talked about Sophie, about how long she and I had lived there, and about how she and her boyfriend had met. We talked about work and about the friends of mine that he liked, and those he thought seemed weird.

He was just as easy to talk to in person—if not more so. I got the impression that I could say anything to him and he wouldn't judge me or make me feel silly as many people would have done if I had shown them my true self. It was always a challenge for me to be able to relate to people once they knew what went on inside of me. Ben seemed like he could handle it.

I looked down at his freckled hand, which was the same size as mine except that his palm was broader.

"Ben," I said, my tone letting on that the conversation was about to turn serious. I didn't want to discourage him so soon, but I also cared enough about him to be up front about where I was emotionally.

"What's up?" he asked, sounding a little hesitant.

"Well, I think you know a little bit about this," I said, "but I just went through a really hard break-up." The understatement of my lifetime.

"Yeah."

"Yeah. So...it's not that I'm not interested in you; I am. I just want you to know that I'm..." I chose my words carefully. *Completely fucked up* seemed a tad too dramatic. Or too honest. "I'm still...healing. I just, I need to take things slow."

"Ok," he said. "I understand." He stopped playing with my hand, but he still held it.

THIRTEEN – OBJECTS IN MIRROR

He seemed slightly deflated, but I think he was relieved that I didn't say "just friends."

Ben left a little while later and I got ready for bed, listening to music softly on my laptop. As I brushed my teeth, I thought about how eleven thirty seemed like a healthy bedtime. I wasn't out late drinking. I wasn't too sick to go out. As I put on my old high-school choir t-shirt and some boxer shorts, I thought about how easy it was holding Ben's hand. I wondered what might come of this but just as soon as I considered it, I felt anxious and so I turned out the light and got under the covers and tried to think of anything else.

Lori McKenna sang to me: "You could burn down this town if they made matches from fear."

I kept dreaming about Chad. I would dream that he kissed me or that I heard he was getting married. I prayed that he would begin to leave my thoughts, now that he was gone from my life. I prayed so hard that I would never see him again.

Perhaps a change of scenery would help and the timing was right for it. Sophie's boyfriend, Nate, was moving to Nashville from Pennsylvania to be with her and I knew they wanted to live together. I loved Sophie and was so thankful for her, but it was nice to be able to move out of that place. I didn't want to have to stare at that same ceiling that covered me on those terrible nights. I didn't want to hear the creak of the screen door and remember how I used to hope it would be Chad coming back. Plus, it was good to get away from Sophie, just for a little while, because she deserved to be happy with Nate and I knew I was a downer. Even the sight of her reminded me of what I had just been through. She didn't need to share it with me any longer.

The condo I'd bought wasn't ready yet so I thought about what else I might look for in the meantime. In the six years that I'd lived on my own, I always had one roommate at a time, always a girl and always in an apartment. I set out to search for something different. I wanted a new experience. I heard about a friend of a friend who lived in a charming old neighborhood and was looking for roommates so I went to meet him and check the place out. The streets were quiet and big trees were scattered through green yards. Justin answered the door in jeans, a white V-neck t-shirt, a silver necklace and a big smile. He had just rented a room to a young musician named Astrud, and the room across the hall from hers had my name all over it, he said.

The house was beautiful too. The living room had a huge picture window that perfectly framed the blooming magnolia tree in the front yard. The kitchen was gray and orange. We painted my room a pale rusty peach color that I had found in a European homes magazine. Justin taught me to "cut in" along the edges of the walls.

He had a recording studio in the third bedroom on the main hall. His bedroom was the sunken den from across the kitchen and there were two bedrooms upstairs, which we used for storage.

The house was just what I needed. There were always people around, all kinds of artists coming and going. Justin built a dining table out of two antique painted wooden doors with a sheet of glass over them; we threw dinner parties several nights a week. Justin didn't believe in microwave ovens so I either had to learn to cook or starve. Now that I had a daily appetite again, I chose to learn how to cook and Astrud taught me. I began to feel at home again, both in my surroundings and in my skin.

September, 2006.

One afternoon, Astrud and I were sitting in the kitchen. She was telling me about her music, about how she had been on some really big tours and how she was once offered a record deal.

"Kimberly, it just got so hard," she confided in me. "I was this teenager, plucked right out of high school and people were saying things to me like, 'You want to be successful?

Write these kinds of songs!' and 'You want to be famous? Lose fifteen pounds, then maybe.' I was scared and frustrated. I love music but that's not how it should be. So, I quit." I could see the devastation in her eyes to see a dream realized and then fall apart with so much still ahead of her.

"And now, I don't know," she continued in her melodic voice. "I want to keep playing but there are all of these bad feelings attached to it. I just, I don't know what else to do with my life."

I could imagine her frustration, but I was also sad to see such talent remain hidden under the surface. Astrud was really quite good and she was only nineteen—too young to be so jaded. Then again, weren't we all?

Astrud hadn't finished high school; she'd dropped out to go on tour. I told her about my high-school and my prom dress, and she told me about a dress she had that she wished she could have worn to her prom. Before we knew it, we were running down the long hallway; bare feet pounding on the dark wood floors, pulling our dresses out of our closets. Laughing at every chance, we put on the dresses, and then we opened a bottle of wine and sat down on the couch. Drinking, chatting and flipping through *W Magazine*, we both watched the sun go down.

"I think you need to keep playing," I told her after we'd been quiet for some time. "I know at first it might not

THIRTEEN – OBJECTS IN MIRROR

feel right or like you're getting anywhere, but you have to give some good feelings a change to replace the bad ones."

I heard my own advice, and I knew that I had to give Ben a little more of a chance. I wanted Astrud to play music again, and I should have the same positive hopes for myself.

Astrud and Justin loved Ben. Most evenings, he would come over and hang out with us in the kitchen while we cooked. With candles lit and freshly picked flowers from the backyard in my favorite glass vase, we'd all sit at the table and eat together like a family. Then, we'd all take an evening walk through the neighborhood, admiring the old houses and the fragrant blossoms on the magnolia trees.

The house on the corner had giant double front doors with metal circles that were held in lions' mouths for doorknobs. There was a small Tudor, my favorite style of house, always the one spot of light and safety in dark fairy tales. However, my favorite house on the street was a white brick home with a sunroom to the side and striped curtains in the window. I imagined the house had a fireplace, original hardwoods floors and a grand piano.

I wasn't ready to stop taking my medication. Though the physical symptoms of my condition had mostly faded, the emotional ones were still there. I felt very alone, despite having people around me constantly. I couldn't imagine very far into the future like I used to. If you had asked me before where I'd like to be in five years, I could have written you a twenty page essay in an hour. Recently, I didn't even think more than a few days ahead of myself—perhaps because the plans that I had for my future had been ripped apart like a shack in a hurricane. Starting from scratch seemed like such an overwhelming task so instead I took a break from planning and dreaming. I focused on enjoying each day and that was enough for now.

One night, Ben asked me if we were a couple. Even though we acted like it and even though I was glad for that, I said no.

October, 2006.

I thought about how the past can become so small. An entire day, 24 separate, heavy hours, becomes the size of a tiny brown leaf falling from a tree. Before you know it, a whole year is just a pile of dead leaves on the ground. The year or so I'd spent in love with Chad was starting to feel so long ago, swept away by the wind. I knew that this year would soon feel far away too.

THIRTEEN – OBJECTS IN MIRROR

A rare urge came over me. I had been doing so well keeping Chad locked only in my dreams, if in my mind at all, that I decided I wanted to see his Myspace page. I had avoided it all along with incredible self-control, but now, a bit more levelheaded, I made the choice to look. Astrud and I drove up to Café Coco and sat on the porch. It had just rained and the streetlights shone in the puddles; the porch seats were damp.

Astrud had never seen Chad before, and I wanted her there with me, partially because I knew that I might need her comfort but also because I wanted her to learn a little bit about the man who had turned me into the fragile thing that she was growing to know so well—the thing that she called, "Little Bird."

I signed into my Myspace account and typed in his name. There wasn't much news, but there were some comments from his band mates and from the girls he used to throw in my face to make me jealous, and there was a blog entry with an update on his life. Astrud and I leaned in and read it together silently. The only part that I remember was the part that changed everything. It said he'd recently made a purchase that had cost more than his car.

He bought her my ring.

I looked at Astrud; this had been a mistake. We closed the computer and drove home. I think I talked the whole way back to the house about how I was "upset but okay."

"I knew this was coming," I said.

Just, maybe, not so soon.

I don't know if it was because he was a man or because he was older and wiser than me, but something about seeing Justin on the back porch strumming his guitar when we got home shook me out of my "I'm okay" mood. I announced the news to him, my voice, knees and hands all shaking at once. Justin put down the guitar and held out his arms. I collapsed against him and he held me as I snorted and slobbered all over his t-shirt; he held me tightly and he continued to hold me until I could breathe again.

November, 2006.

Nashville began to get attention from some high-end fashion stores, and when one of the new stores opened I was thrilled to get a great job offer from them. Oh, how fun it was to get to wear these kinds of clothes! I had just turned twenty-four but I still felt like I was playing dress up in my pencil skirts and tailored suit jackets. I would wear the black, brown and white wool poplin pencil skirt with brown boots. I wore the camel one that hugged my bottom perfectly with

THIRTEEN – OBJECTS IN MIRROR

brown argyle knee socks and booties. I wore the black skirt with a little vest and my favorite black peep toe pumps that I had to kick off as soon as we locked the doors to clean the store.

I had more trouble selling at the new store. The competition was fierce and the other sales associates had already established clientele. Every day, I felt like I was falling just short. I had clients stolen from under me, even though I helped them choose three thousand dollars worth of the most beautiful clothes that I'd ever seen, because they had a relationship with another stylist.

That's what we were called—stylists. I loved the title but I didn't feel like I was being allowed to live up to the name with terms like "items-per-sale" and "dollars-per-hour" constantly shoved down my throat. Despite my trouble on the sales floor, I adored the management staff and wanted so badly to be one of them. Olivia, in particular, reminded me so much of myself. She had a little more in the quirky department and a little less in the well-organized section; however, we became fast friends who complemented each other well.

Liv, as I took to calling her immediately, was taller than me and her hair was cut in a blonde bob with side swept bangs. She was always in the highest and most amazing shoes. She brought with her an arsenal of hilarious phrases like "I miss your face!" and "I can't even take it right now!" and the almost-overuse of the word "cute." Everything she said was accompanied by a smile that said, "You know you love me," and a train of proverbial exclamation points.

I loved her immensely.

Before New Year's, I dyed my long hair from blonde to brown, which is the color that I always go to when I want to take life more seriously. It went with my new wardrobe and my new attitude. I went out with more eligible guys that I met while I was sober but none of them stuck. Astrud, Ben and I hung out a lot, but I stopped letting Ben kiss me. Neither of us had been able to commit after my original "no," and we seemed to be better as friends. I dated the other guys in part to make him jealous, but I honestly was just trying to move forward in life, and then, just like that, life began to move forward with me.

14
Guilty

February, 2007.

One day in February, I was helping one of Nashville's best wardrobe stylists pull some clothes for one of her clients. Liv and I were the only girls on the sales floor and there weren't any other customers in the store so I had a chance to talk to the stylist more than usual as she browsed.

"I'd actually really like to get into styling," I told her. "If you ever need help with anything, I'd love to get some experience." I said it casually, but I felt like I was going out on a limb.

The days of dressing my Barbies in the one-of-a-kind Barbie clothes that my grandmother's friend had made had been flooding back to me lately, along with the living room fashion shows that I'd put on with Meredith.

"Really! That's great! I don't usually need much help but there are some jobs that I pass on because of scheduling or budget. Give me your number, I'd be happy to pass some of those calls along to you."

It was a promise for more than I could have hoped. I was surprised when I got a call from her not even two weeks later.

"I'm styling on *Nashville Star* and I could use an intern. I can't pay you but it's just two days a week. Are you interested?"

Breathe. Don't scream.

"Yes!"

"Can you start Wednesday?"

"YES!"

I didn't want to lose my hours at the store so my manager scheduled me every day from Friday to Tuesday. I had Nashville Star dress rehearsals on Wednesdays and the live show was filmed on Thursdays. I helped her unpack the clothes, steam them, decide which outfit was right for each contestant and pack up everything again.

When I had free time before or after a shift at the store, I met the contestants for fittings or helped by doing

FOURTEEN - GUILTY

returns. Between both jobs, I had never worked so hard in all my life. I didn't care one bit that I wasn't being paid for the show. This was my foot in the door.

One week I had to miss the show because Liv and I were going to New York for fashion week. We didn't actually go to the fashion shows, though we did walk by the big white tent in Bryant Park. They televised the shows in the city so we watched some of our favorites from our hotel room at the Chelsea Inn.

Oh, that Reem Acra dress is incredible!

Phillip Lim has such vision for fall!

The hotel was a little piece of heaven, where the rooms looked like your grandma's house and every morning we got a complimentary coffee and pastries from the café downstairs. I sat in the window seat and watched the morning sea of people that were below while Liv messed with her hair and tried to wake up. Liv, the doll, was so not a morning person.

This was the first time I'd been to New York since my teenage years when we saw *Rent* and Times Square and FAO Schwartz. This trip was completely different. We saw Prada and Bloomingdales and went to Cafeteria and La Petite Abielle.

The stylist that I was interning for made good use of my trip by having me stop by a designer's studio to pick out handmade leather pieces to bring back on loan. The designer made stuff for Sheryl Crow, Lenny Kravitz and designed the American flag corset and red leather pants that Britney Spears once wore on the cover of *Rolling Stone*.

I lugged the heavy shopping bag of $8,000 worth of leather goods all the way back to Nashville, and I had a proud moment when one of the contestants wore a pair of pants that I had chosen on the show a few weeks later. I enjoyed playing an important role behind the scenes.

The student intern on the show and I became the cool kids at lunch; our table filled up quickly with other members of the production team. I spent most of my time doing whatever was needed, even if it was running out to the mall last minute to get a contestant a thong because she showed up for the taping not wearing any underwear at all. By the end of the season, I was allowed on stage during commercial breaks to straighten one of the contestant's top or lint roll a jacket.

It was like summer camp—we were all so sad to see it end after the finale, but after that I started getting work on short films and music videos. Also, I heard a rumor that one of the managers at the boutique where I had done much better in sales had put in his two weeks notice. I called Taryn right away and told her that I wanted the job. She was willing to interview me, but she wanted me to know that there was

FOURTEEN - GUILTY

another employee up for it; my only concern was that the other candidate was still with the company and I wasn't. I knew that I had her beat in skill, and in the end, I got the job.

I was so glad to leave the competitive sales atmosphere in which I was struggling. I would miss my new friends and the clothes, but I knew Liv and I would remain friends no matter what.

The stylist that I'd been working with came in to the store often, and she asked me to assist her on a few projects that she had coming up. My professional life was falling gently into place while nothing in my romantic life had changed much. Ben had been in the audience at *Nashville Star* every single week, and I don't think it's because he liked the show that much.

May, 2007.

Astrud and I had moved out of the house and into our own apartment, where we'd met some new neighbors we were hanging out with. Phil and Zane had just moved in to the building across from ours. Phil, a thin guy with very short hair and narrow eyes, was a keyboard player from Maryland. Zane was a rocker from Manchester, England. He was not much taller than Ben with long, wild, curly dark hair and a constant 5 o'clock shadow; he wore *Guns-N-Roses* t-shirts with frayed vests and ripped jeans painted with American flag stripes.

Phil and Zane were new to Nashville, having met each other while working on a cruise ship and decided to move together to pursue music individually. When we first met them, I thought Phil was cute, but as I got to know them, I became fascinated with Zane. Maybe it was the accent or the deep and tangled conversations in which we would find ourselves. However, I didn't necessarily think of either of them romantically.

I found myself more hung up on Ben than ever. I was sleeping in his yellow t-shirt every night. I was sleeping at his house sometimes too, after staying up late watching TV with him. We still weren't kissing, though I knew we both wanted to. If he couldn't commit to me, then I wasn't willing to give him that.

I guess holding out worked. I went to visit my parents, and the night I got back, Ben asked me to come over. I told him that I'd told my mom that I had feelings for him. I said it kind of nonchalantly, assuming of course that I was just there to watch TV, which is what we were doing as usual.

"I like you, too," he said.

I didn't take my eyes off *Entourage*.

"Yes, as a good friend, of course," I said.

I was used to this.

FOURTEEN - GUILTY

"While you were gone," he said, "I was thinking that I wouldn't mind being your boyfriend."

"What!?" Now I was paying attention.

"Yeah, I mean like that would be okay with me. If you were still interested or whatever."

"Seriously? Are you sure about this?" I asked.

"Yes. I told Jimmy," he replied.

Oh, well, if your best friend knows, it must be for real.

"Wow. Okay. I mean, yes, I still want that." I told him. "Yes!"

Zane and I went out for Mexican food the next day. I talked of my new "boyfriend" and how I knew he would finally commit some day. Zane laughed at me; he didn't really believe in monogamy, but he'd never been in love.

The next night Sophie was singing background vocals at a bar we called Longshots. It was actually called "The Longshot," but no one ever picked up on that. A girl that Sophie knew from school, Kellie, asked Sophie to sing with her band on Thursday nights. Ben, Astrud, and I went and sat at a high four top table. Longshots was a sports bar so there were flat screen TVs and sports team paraphernalia decorating the primary-blue walls.

The band had already started by the time we arrived, and they were playing "Save a Horse, Ride a Cowboy." I ordered a Jack-and-diet and the warmth of the liquor was no match for my heart. I was on cloud nine. Ben held my hand. We all laughed and shouted over the band or sang along until they had played every song that they knew, and by then the bar was closing anyway.

Now that he was my boyfriend, Ben took me on real dates. He dressed up and I dressed up and he brought me a dozen hot pink roses. He drove us to a fancy restaurant that I'd never been to before. The only difference in our relationship since we made it official was that I actually felt that he was holding back. I wasn't staying at his house at all. I saw him less often and he was less physically affectionate. This was so unlike us.

It must be because he wants to do this right, I thought, *or maybe he's scared.*

Always making excuses for a man's shortcomings.

Some days, Ben was proving to be a very good boyfriend. He would call to "check on me." He was considerate, making sure that I knew when he had plans with the guys; he surprised me, but other times I felt like he was somewhere else completely—not holding my hand or showing up really late when we had plans to meet out somewhere.

I tried to talk to him about it.

"I know," he said. "I'll do better."

FOURTEEN - GUILTY

But he didn't. It got worse. On the Fourth of July, my favorite holiday, he told me that he'd meet me at the bar downtown instead of riding there with me. He came in late; he was already drunk and he made it clear that he had no interest in being there or being there with me.

I didn't complain at the karaoke bar later that week when he sat with the two friends that he'd brought and who I had never met before—somewhere else in the room. Zane sat on my lap and I pretended to be "squished" and made a comment about Ben being nearby.

"He won't care, it's me," Zane said in his incredible English accent.

"He wouldn't care anyway," I said.

I let him sit there and we shared each other's drinks. I thought if I could make Ben jealous, he would snap out of it, but he didn't.

Then, one night, Zane and Phil came over. Phil left early while Zane and I sat on my bed talking. I loved talking with Zane; he was so smart and though his viewpoints on a lot of things were different from mine, we always respected the other, realizing that—in part—it was our differences that made our talks so interesting. As the talking wound down and we grew tired, we lay next to each other on top of the covers and whispered at a slower pace. Then, he kissed me.

It didn't surprise me that he did. It did surprise me how much I liked it. He kissed me again and I thought about Ben and I pushed him away and he left.

But I thought about him all the next day and I knew that I wanted more of Zane. He sent me a text message that said he knew he should be sorry but he wasn't. Sophie and I were shopping in Hillsboro Village and I hadn't taken my sunglasses off. In and out of the shops, I didn't take them off. I knew that if she took one glance into my eyes, they would scream, "I'm guilty!"

He came over again after Sophie's show at Longshots that Thursday. He left me with teeth marks imprinted on my arm.

I knew this was not the way to fix things with Ben so I talked to him about how I was feeling unfulfilled in our relationship. He listened and texted me the next day, "I like you like a fat kid likes cake," and then he took me to dinner with his parents.

I didn't know if it was enough, and I didn't know if I could stay away from Zane. I was plagued by guilt. Honestly, I knew it was over with Ben. He had no interest in fixing our relationship and I was basically having an affair.

Zane was over every night. Usually, he came to my window to see what I was doing. It was apparent that Ben

FOURTEEN - GUILTY

was not making time for me since I was always home doing nothing. Zane and I would even kiss at the door when he left and I wondered if Ben would show up and catch us. Maybe I wanted him to—actually not maybe. Yes, I wanted him to. I didn't want to hurt him, but I wanted him to pay more attention to me like Zane was.

But I tended not to date men who ever showed up for me.

Finally, I let Zane in. That's when I knew it was really over with Ben. Even if I preferred to be with Ben, I knew that it wasn't working so I was attempting to protect myself by making other plans. It didn't feel like I was being protected though. It felt like I was making a mess.

I needed to get away so I went and stayed at a friend's house just outside of town. We smoked pot on the patio and I kept my cell phone off the whole weekend. I smoked very rarely and I'd never been that high. I hung out on the outdoor lounge for hours without moving, hovering somewhere above myself in the haze.

On Sunday, I went back to Nashville and straight to Ben's place in my white linen dress. I was still in a bit of a daze and much tanner from baking in the sun. I knew we had to talk about things but I had no idea what I was going to say. Before I could say anything at all, Ben broke up with me. I was hurt but not devastated. Maybe I was even a little relieved. I was more worried about losing my friend than anything else—as was he—but my heart weighed heavy in my chest. I'd loved him for a year. He saved me from myself when I was so broken, and now, after barely giving it a real shot, it was over. I slept on Sophie's couch that night, afraid that the anxiety would return.

I avoided Ben and kept seeing Zane. I needed space to grieve if there was going to be any hope of keeping a friendship with Ben. Then, Ben found out about Zane. He called me drunk in the middle of the night to announce that he knew, and then he came over to talk about it. He wasn't angry, which was precisely the problem, but he was hurt and he had lost his trust in me. I understood and I deserved that.

I told him that I needed some time to get over him. Despite my disrespectful actions, I really cared about him. I needed to be away from him until I was ready to be his friend again. Just his friend; I still believed that was possible.

One day I got a text from Zane that he had spent the previous night in the hospital. He'd been having headaches lately that were becoming increasingly worse. It got so bad that Phil, his roommate, had taken him to the ER. They were waiting on test results but Zane said the doctors thought he had a brain tumor. I went to see him on my lunch break, then

FOURTEEN - GUILTY

again after work, and again the next night. Phil was asleep on the cot in Zane's tiny room. I lay on the bed next to Zane, his head in the nook of my shoulder, and I played with his long curly hair. He was wearing the silver bracelet that I'd brought him.

It was a brain tumor, the doctors told him, and he made plans to go home to England to have his surgery. He was released from the hospital the next day, Friday, and would be leaving on Monday for England. Friday night, I went over to Phil and Zane's for dinner and then Zane and I watched a movie and fell asleep on his bed—his head in my lap.

I took Saturday off work to help Zane run errands; most of the errands were for him to tie up a few things but one stop was for me. I was checking out storage units. The condo that I had bought when I was with Chad was almost complete, and I didn't know if I was moving into it or into another apartment of my own. I did know that I was ready to live alone. Metamorphosis was becoming a habit for me. When my heart was broken, I changed everything about myself and my scenery in order to mend it.

After our errands, Zane and I watched movies all afternoon and dozed off for a little while. I was somewhere between asleep and awake when the balloon that he brought home from the hospital caught my eye as it danced in the draft from the fan and I watched it for a minute. As sleep began to overtake me, my half-open eyes caught a glimpse of a woman in his mirror.

I think it was an angel.

15
Apartment Twelve

The butterfly in reverse here is me.
Counting Crows

August, 2007.

The first week that Zane was gone I stayed in his room a few nights. There I was surrounded by his scent and his spirit. I loved that the DVDs were alphabetized and it included both Disney titles and live rock concerts. I loved the three pairs of cowboy boots that lined up in his closet.

I knew better than to romanticize our relationship. Knowing myself, my imagination could easily take us from being close friends to being soul mates torn apart by a big ocean and a little tumor—all in a matter of days. I worked hard to remember what was real; we were friends. However, I couldn't help but think about the similarities between Chase and Zane. Eyeliner, velvet, claiming an unconcern for the opinions of others and a battle with a sort of darkness that no one else could see. Even his room: Zane's mattress was on the bare floor like in the apartment that I shared with Chase in my imaginations. He had essentially no furniture; a few books, DVDs, guitar, loud music.

Somehow, I always end up in these rooms alone.

Remember, I told myself, *he's not the guy in your dreams. He is a real person with needs and faults and you can love him, but you're not right for each other.*

Even though I didn't know what was right for me, I knew it wasn't him.

The condo that I'd bought, my would-have-been "home" with Chad, was almost completed and I couldn't afford to live there. I talked with four mortgage brokers who all said that my credit was good but that I didn't make enough to get approved for the loan on my own. I envisioned a man-behind-the-curtain scene at the bank and a loud voice saying that, "She might be responsible but she's gone overboard with the credit cards and she makes squat!" The little man, on the other hand, in his striped button down shirt sat

FIFTEEN – APARTMENT TWELVE

at a wooden desk and stared at all of my financial failures in one neat little folder.

I should have been living in that condo, cozying up on the couch with my husband, rather than in this mess alone.

Damn Chad.

Damn him, damn him, damn him!

September, 2007.

In September I went home to Westville and stopped by Chase's house to see his mom. I sat on the couch and talked with her and cried. The last time that I'd been there, I wouldn't go into his room. I hadn't been ready, but this time I was.

"Spend as much time in there as you need, Kit, sweetheart," she said. "And just let me know if there is anything you'd like to have."

I looked for his notes from me but couldn't find them. He wouldn't have gotten rid of them, would he? I did find some pictures of us that I didn't have so I took them. I looked for his *Stone Temple Pilots* t-shirt, too, but didn't find it.

When I came back out, his mom handed me a small gray box that said "Shine" on the lid like the tattoo on the back of my neck that I'd gotten for him that August, on the anniversary of his death. As I was lifting the lid, I realized what I was about to see—a small packet of his ashes.

She was giving me part of Chase, an actual part of him. I was unable to articulate how much that meant to me, but I hoped my tears showed it.

November, 2007.

I sold the condo and was free from the future Chad and I had planned, and I even got to keep the profit. I patted myself on the back for being smart enough to put only my name on the contract. Now I could decide for myself where I wanted to live, and I was ready to have my own place. Sure, it was more expensive to live without a roommate, but I needed my own space. I needed a place that I wouldn't want to run away from, somewhere to spread my wings and to take care of myself. The property manager of a complex in the neighborhood where Kellie and Sophie lived showed me the most beautiful apartment that I'd ever seen.

Apartment Twelve.

I loved it more than any fancy new condo.

It had three spacious rooms. The kitchen was large enough for a little cafe table and chairs, and I had shining granite countertops and warm blush-colored tile. The huge living room and bedroom floors were hardwood and each

FIFTEEN – APARTMENT TWELVE

room had an old painted radiator. Crown molding ran throughout the place and there were windows on every wall. Never before had I let so much light into my life. I used to cover my windows with heavy curtains—never drawn. Now I danced in the sunlight on my hardwood floors.

I put the farmhouse dining table with four of its six curved cream-colored Belini chairs at the end of the living room close to the kitchen. I painted a yard sale table light pink and put it with the other two chairs in the corner of the kitchen under the big pink and green painting that read, "I gave her roses and she blames me for the thorns."

Then, there was the bedroom. Oh, the bedroom! I found a wooden nightstand at an antique mall and replaced the knob on the drawer with a heavy round black and white striped treasure. The bottom of it held three years worth of *Vogue* Magazines. It sat atop a cream shag rug that my bare feet would hit first thing every morning. When I could afford it, I bought the dreamiest bedding. Gray and tufted with pillow shams to match.

This is my bed, I thought. *No one else belongs. There's no room here to miss anyone.* I stopped sleeping on the right side and slept smack dab in the middle, and I slept like a baby.

I turned twenty-five the week after I moved in. I always knew that I would not be the girl having the quarter life crisis. That had come to pass, and even the romantic crises were at bay for now.

And it wasn't just the apartment. I opened the windows to my life and let the sun shine in. My career, my social life, my spiritual life and my physical health all flourished despite the lack of activity in my love life, which used to be the center of all things. I was loving myself and, after all, that really should be enough.

My career grew slowly and steadily. I took an administrative job in marketing, which helped me to develop a steady daily routine and gave me more funds to build my styling business. I was booking more gigs and styling artists on music video shoots and models on fashion photo shoots and I worked backstage at the CMT Awards. I began to build a solid multi-media portfolio for myself.

I had still been attending the wonderful, young and active church that I found with Lacey when I moved back from L.A., but aside from sitting on a folding chair in the downtown music venue where we met each Sunday morning, I had hardly been a member of the church community. Now, I began to make friends at church and grow in my own faith. I used to compartmentalize God. Although I still struggled with this, knowing that I needed to let God into the darkest and scariest corners of my heart, but I was getting

FIFTEEN – APARTMENT TWELVE

better and better at it and I was led by the example of my church family.

I lived by that old Girl Scout song, "make new friends but keep the old, one is silver and the other's gold." Since our days at Longshots, Kellie, Sophie and I had developed a close, intimate friendship. Three's company and we were a perfect support system for each other through what was happening in each of our lives. I was more different from each of them than any other close friend that I'd had, and sometimes it felt like it was hard for them to understand me; regardless, they unfailingly supported everything that I did.

Kellie and her boyfriend who had been the drummer for the Longshot's band broke up after five years of dating. He had been Kellie's first and only boyfriend, and she was experimenting now with dating casually and being on her own. As an assistant to a booking agent at a major talent company, she began to discover that she had the mind of an agent. She started working with new artists and producers, helping them to develop their talents and ideas in the hopes that they would soon be her own clients.

Sophie and one of the guitarists for the band began dating much in the same way that you notice a house being built on your drive to work—slowly, then suddenly. They fell into a beautiful, respectful and mad love and began to plan a wedding.

New friends were coming into my life from many different places. Aside from my church friends, there was a guy from my partying and dancing days. We both had cut back on the partying and found that we had much else in common too, particularly our taste in men. A new girlfriend worked for the salon where I had been getting my hair done. She turned me back to my favorite shade of blonde. She was younger and livelier than me, always so enthusiastic about what I had to tell her or what was new in her own life. She was completely unafraid of what anyone thought of her, and that's probably because one would have had to search very, very hard to find anything bad to say about her.

There were others too. I remembered learning from my favorite professor at Belmont to "surround yourself with people who are better than you," and I was now living that mantra. I found myself amongst strong and admirable people who built me up and I wanted to build them up too.

For Christmas, Mom asked my brother and me to search for some way to volunteer or to do something positive in the community as her gift. I wanted to find a cause that I was passionate about and to utilize my talent and resources in whatever it was that I decided to do. After seeing a girl that I had worked with battle cancer and now that Zane had cancer too, I had become more aware of the existence of

FIFTEEN – APARTMENT TWELVE

cancer in young adults as a real and too common occurrence. I began to learn more about the statistics and challenges that affected this particular group, and this became my cause of choice. My friends jumped in to help and we planned a concert/fashion show event for an organization that was called *Stupid Cancer,* which helped young adults with cancer to network with one another, both online and via social gatherings, and provided them with resources and other support.

The organization's founder came to Nashville from New York to attend our event and to give a little speech. My friends and I were thrilled with the turnout; there were about three hundred people in the small music venue, all people who were there to see the bands, to support their survivor friends or to take in the fashion show. The event sparked a relationship between the *Stupid Cancer* organization and the young adult cancer community in Nashville, and it was from that moment that our team decided to make the concert/fashion show an annual event.

I was much thinner than I had been in LA., and I was more filled out than I had been when I was sick. Although I was happy with my size, I still wasn't using my gym membership one bit so I hired a personal trainer for a month to kick start a more active lifestyle. I realized that not only did I begin to shape my body, but I also learned that I really liked exercising. Kellie and I started indoor rock climbing, and I became convinced that I was born to climb. I loved the rush, the challenge and the pain that came the next day. I picked up yoga again too, and I ran and weight trained, and I loved every minute of it. Ok, everything but the walking lunges.

I made an effort to keep all of my newfound strengths as lifelong habits. I didn't want to work out for a few weeks and then let it go. I didn't want to raise awareness for cancer at one event and then move on. This was the life that I was building for myself. These were solid bricks in my foundation.

As I'd hoped, one day I realized that I missed having Ben as my friend—just my friend. Since our break up, he had been calling every now and then and leaving me voicemails: *Hello, I hope all is well, call me when you're ready.* I was ready to be his friend but I was hesitant to move back into even that relationship with him. I was afraid that if I let him back into my life that the feelings would come back too. As a result, I decided to take things easy. We had dinner one night, and then a phone conversation a few weeks later. Little by little I found a comfort with our friendship being just that and nothing more, and that our friendship would never be more was no longer a sad thing.

FIFTEEN – APARTMENT TWELVE

So what about dating? I wasn't ignoring the male gender by any means, and I wasn't deliberately fasting from dating, but I was so focused on caring for myself that there wasn't as much of me available to give to each of the Joe Nobodies who came along. I liked many of the guys that I went out with, a few of them could have been "The One," however, nothing clicked and none of them held my attention for long or I didn't hold theirs for whatever reason. At least now, I was looking forward again.

I knew that I'd come a long way, but I didn't realize how far until one blazing August day when I met Blake.

16
The Sky Has Good Intentions

August, 2008.

Most days at the marketing office I wore jeans and flats, cotton tank tops and cardigans, but on that day I had a big meeting so I wore the fancy camel pencil skirt suit. I had missed wearing my beautiful adult clothes, anyway. After work, I was meeting Sophie and Kellie for dinner at our favorite restaurant, where we'd been going a couple of nights a week since the beginning of summer. They had cheap sushi, good cocktails and cute bartenders, one in particular I had been watching. I loved his curly brown hair, his bright smile and his jeans rolled up at the ankles.

He never seemed to recognize me from one night to the next, but we kept going back and I kept hoping that on

SIXTEEN – THE SKY HAS GOOD INTENTIONS

one of these days he might speak to me. That night, he was standing at the hostess stand when I walked in, before Sophie or Kellie had gotten there.

"Three please, outside if you have a table open," I said to the hostess. The bartender was watching me and smiling. He was deliciously tall. I smiled back at him but then looked right back at the hostess. I had no reason to expect him to speak to me.

"You look familiar," he said. His voice was like lying in a hammock on a spring day—warm sun, cool breeze.

"I come here a lot," I replied, trying to hide what I was actually thinking: *I cannot believe you don't recognize me from sitting on that bar stool right there four nights a week, you idiot.*

"I'm Blake," he said, holding out his hand and shaking mine solidly. I was impressed by his confidence.

"Kimberly," I said.

"Nice to meet you," he replied.

I followed the hostess to a table outside, and Kellie and Sophie arrived shortly thereafter. We filled each other in on the happenings of our workday and I told them both about how the hot bartender finally spoke to me and that I wondered if there might have been more he wanted to say.

"Well, that's progress, for sure!" Sophie said.

"I wish I'd been here to see it," Kellie added.

I loved these girls with all my heart.

A few nights later, Kellie and I were leaving Hamilton's after hanging out with a group of her work friends when I suggested that we stop to see if the cute bartender was working. It was on the way home, it wasn't that late and I really thought he might ask for my number when given the chance. Kellie was tired but she agreed.

I walked tall in my cream t-strap heels, pink satin top and cream belt, and dark skinny jeans. We sat at the bar and ordered a blackberry mojito and a glass of wine. Blake recognized me right away, for the first time, and kept coming over to chat. He wanted to hear all about the photo shoot that I'd worked on that day.

Unfortunately, he still hadn't asked for my number or a date or my hand in marriage, and my drink was getting low.

"Sorry," Kellie said quietly when he was off checking on the one table he still had. "Time to go to bed. If he's gonna ask, he will. We gotta go."

I nodded and took one last sip of my sweet fruity mojito, leaving the dewy glass on the wood bar. We pushed back from our stools and slung our purses over our shoulders. Blake got it that we were leaving and he came back over to us.

SIXTEEN – THE SKY HAS GOOD INTENTIONS

"Hey, I'm moving into a new house next week. My old roommate..." and he went into a story that was longer than it needed to be, and I wasn't sure where he was going with it. He could see the lost, "wrap it up, buddy" look in my eye, and then he cut to the chase. "Well, we're having a housewarming party and I'd love it if you would come."

He glanced in Kellie's direction, politely including her.

"Can I get your number? I'll text you the info."

"Sure!" I was thrilled.

I told him my number and we were gone.

I wondered if he'd call. I wondered if there really was a party.

Blake did text me. He wrote, "Hey! I'm getting off work and sitting here with some friends. You should come." I didn't have his number in my phone yet so I found it charmingly appropriate to write back, "Who's this?"

Yeah, I was playing the game.

"Oh, sorry, this is Blake," he replied.

"Oh, hey!" I said. "Yeah, I think I can come by. Thirty minutes?"

I picked out an outfit that was cute but didn't scream trying-too-hard, shorts and a black sleeveless blouse with lilac swirls, and added a touch of makeup. Then, I rode the scooter that I had bought at the beginning of summer down

Belmont Boulevard toward the restaurant, the cool breeze calming my nerves. I parked across the street from the patio and shook my hair out of the helmet before storing the helmet in the seat. I liked to imagine that I was in slow motion when I did this, but I probably looked dumb.

I crossed the street and saw Blake sitting on the patio with three friends, staring with eyes wide.

"No way, that's yours?" he asked.

"Yeah," I laughed.

"That is so hot."

I found out that Blake was in Green Peace and rode only a bicycle so he was more impressed with my nod to the environment than my sexy hair shaking moves.

He stayed across the big round table from me and I sat near some of his friends. I shook hands with his friends and asked getting-to-know-you type questions. I didn't want to act like that I was there just for him. I was out to make some new friends. No big deal.

After a drink or two, we decided to move on to another bar where we could play darts. Blake rode his bike and I rode the scooter. Somewhere in the half mile stretch between bars, I decided that I liked Blake. To start, he was better looking than any guy that I'd dated and so far. Also I'd learned that he went to college at the Art Institute in L.A., he was an artist who painted and sketched, and his degree was

SIXTEEN – THE SKY HAS GOOD INTENTIONS

in culinary arts, meaning that he could cook. All of it thrilled me.

We played darts at the bar, girls against guys, drinking and laughing. The girls won in part because, for no good reason at all, I was and always have been excellent at darts. I don't even know how to keep score. I just aim and throw really well.

Blake went to get another drink and I sat on a stool smiling and sipping my rum and Diet Coke as his friend cleaned the scoreboard. When Blake returned, he announced that he'd made a few jukebox selections for us. First up was a *Counting Crows* song. He was throwing darts straight at my heart.

We started playing again, this time with Blake and me on the same team. I threw my three red-winged darts, good but not my best, and then I stepped back and smiled.

"Wow, okay," he said. "You can be on my team anytime."

His next song selection came on. It was *Queen's* "Bohemian Rhapsody," a song that is absolutely one-hundred-percent impossible not to sing along to. Our game halted for seven minutes of Blake leading the entire bar in a rowdy, laughter-filled sing-along. This was serious.

We moved from the bar to Blake's house, just down the street. Then the drinking really began. We did vodka-

and-orange-juice shots in a kitchen decorated with some of his art and I taught some yoga moves to his friends in the living room. Looking back, this is proof that I was drunk. Living room yoga is not really great first date behavior, but then again, I was making a good effort to display to him some of my best qualities: I always win at darts and my plow pose is fantastic.

Later, somewhere in the vodka-and-orange-juice haze, I found myself in the kitchen with Blake. It had to be four in the morning. Easily, he reached out and put his arms around my waist and pulled me to him. He smiled that brilliant and invigorating smile and he kissed me. It was long and it was soft, but it was passionate. It was perfect.

When we stopped, I leaned back and looked at him. It was in these moments that I gave too much away. I was suddenly unafraid to show that I was happy, smiling with my mouth and with my eyes. I looked at him without really seeing as I searched for his soul behind his eyes. Then I saw that his face didn't mirror mine. He was smiling, but it was a funny smile, his eyes squinty. He looked...terrified!

"What's wrong?" I asked, pulling back from his hold a bit. It *was* still a smile. "Why do you look so scared?"

"I am. I am scared," he said.

"Well, don't be, you're freaking me out. Just kiss me again."

SIXTEEN – THE SKY HAS GOOD INTENTIONS

He gladly did.

Was there really a crack in his confident facade? Didn't he know how amazing he was? Why would he be so nervous kissing a girl? I decided that I liked that his confident act wasn't seamless. It was a good thing that he wasn't full of himself.

"I have to tell you something," he said suddenly, shaking me out of my analysis of his personality.

"Okay." He still held me while he leaned against the kitchen counter.

"I knew who you were when I asked your name. I've been watching you all summer. And I never thought in a million years that you would speak to me, let alone be here, now. With me."

"Oh!" I looked away while absorbing this new and fascinating information, deciding whether to make a confession of my own. *Go for it*, my heart said, my heart always said.

"I watched you all summer too. I thought you never noticed me. You never looked at me, you never spoke to me."

"I know. I didn't know what to say. I didn't know how..."

We both seemed pleased with the outcome of our situation.

We kissed some more and then we crashed. Wow, a whole three hours of sleep. But the next day every yawn was followed by a smile.

Over the next few months, I learned some interesting things from Blake. Who would have guessed that I liked green peppers on my pizza or that offshore drilling was preventing the US from looking for alternative sources for fuel as eagerly as we should be? He called every day while I was in Pittsburgh visiting Meredith. He called while he was out for a walk, just thinking of me. He called while he was on his way to a protest downtown, save-the-trees-something.

Sometimes he wouldn't call for a few days and I would think, *Here it is. I knew it.* But then he would call and chat just like normal, ask me to come over or to go climbing or for a bike ride. He always had extra bikes at his house. I hadn't been on a bike since childhood, but one night I decided that he'd been working so hard and I should throw him a bone. I rode the bike.

It was cold so I wore boots and a sweater and some random hat that had been in my trunk on its way to Goodwill. We rode all over Vanderbilt's campus, then up and down a parking garage ramp. I was more comfortable there with no cars in the parking garage. I rode up and down, up and down, and Blake just watched. I rode closer to him and

SIXTEEN – THE SKY HAS GOOD INTENTIONS

smiled. I wanted him to know that I could do this. I could be a bicyclist. Kind of.

"You look so fucking sexy on that bike with your little hat on," he said.

I laughed. I thought that I probably looked pathetic. They say you don't forget how to ride a bike, but really you sort of do.

One night he called from downtown. He was at a show with some friends and was about to ride his bike up to Dragon Park, where he was usually found when not working and where I'd been with him a couple of times lately. I drove over to meet him, and sat on one of the swings and waited.

I knew it would take his bike longer than my car to get there but I felt like I'd waited forever on that swing. His bike didn't come around the bend in the path, his fedora lit in the moonlight. How long had I been sitting there? Forty minutes? Fifty? I went back to the car and checked my phone. He hadn't called. I didn't care enough to call. Those times he would disappear for a few days, he always had an excuse: "My friend was in trouble," or "I got in a fight with my brother," or "I lost my phone." I didn't want to have to check up on him and I didn't want to hear any excuses so I drove home, listening to a Pink song that I loved: "You're the swing set and I'm the kid that falls."

He called the next day to tell me he had fallen downtown and broken his leg. He asked if I would pick him up from the hospital in a few hours. He called again when he was about to be discharged and I left work early to go get him. I took him to the pharmacy to get his prescription and I loaned him twenty bucks for it. He had paid his ER co-pay, a couple of hundred dollars, in cash at the hospital. That was all he had for the week. At least he had health insurance. I bought us dinner and then I told him to call me if he needed anything before I headed home. On my drive home and in the car, I wondered to myself what we were. We were dating but it had been months and I wasn't sure what he wanted from me. I knew what I wanted from him, but did I trust him? Did I believe that he could give me what I wanted?

Without the ability to walk, he couldn't work so he lost his serving job. He moved all of his stuff, which wasn't very much, into his mom's apartment, and his roommates who had been his only friends were no longer his friends for whatever reason. The man had nothing.

Kellie called and I was telling her what had happened to Blake and why he hadn't shown up at the swings.

"Kim, he is so stupid! He does all this stupid stuff and you just go, 'la la la whatever.' I dated someone like him for

SIXTEEN – THE SKY HAS GOOD INTENTIONS

five years. He's just like Aaron! He's immature and stupid and you're wasting your time!" Kellie isn't one for subtlety.

"Kel, he's not like Aaron though. I can see how you think that and yes, he was stupid for climbing a bridge and falling and breaking his leg, but he is different than he was and he wants to continue to improve his life."

"Stop defending him!"

She made me feel like I had to defend myself.

"I'm not, I said I know he was stupid, but that isn't all that's there. Plus, we're taking it slow. I'm protecting myself! What's wrong with that?"

We went on like this for a few minutes. She and I had never fought like this before. I couldn't believe that she had taken such a strong stance against him that in two years of friendship this would be the topic of our first fight.

"Well, do whatever you want of course, and I love you, but I do not think this is smart," she said and then we agreed to disagree and we both hung up the phone upset.

I hate to say this but I wasn't really sad to see him hit rock bottom. From what I'd witnessed, he had some growing up to do. Sometimes having everything taken from you can force you to make the needed changes in your life. We started talking every day and hanging out much more often. He had nothing else to do and no one else to see, after all.

He was still on crutches when I was housesitting at the Jamison's, and he came over and cooked dinner. He made pasta with sun-dried tomatoes and a tossed salad with strawberries. The meal was delicious and the presentation was brilliant.

We sat at the big round dining table and talked until well after the food was gone. He told me what he remembered from his childhood in New Orleans. He shared some of his favorite memories from L.A. We discovered that he'd worked at a restaurant in Venice Beach where I knew the chef. I told him about my journey to Nashville, what my hometown was like, and about my faith. He asked more about my church and my beliefs, and I invited him to come to church with me sometime. I told him that I had once lost everything I had too, and that I think that can be God's way of building walls around us to force us to look up at Him.

"It's been so long since I've had faith," Blake said, "I wouldn't know what to do with it if I found it again."

At least he was thinking about it.

Then we sat in front of the fireplace for a while, sometimes talking and sometimes silent, and he said twice what a nice time he'd had.

On my last night of house-sitting at the Jamison's, I was having some friends over for a dinner party. I invited

SIXTEEN – THE SKY HAS GOOD INTENTIONS

Blake and asked him if he'd help me cook. I knew Kellie was coming and decided it best not to tell her that Blake would be there. She's generally a polite person so I knew that she'd stay quiet or avoid him and deal with me later.

I picked up Blake when I got off work and we went to the store for fresh pork tenderloin and chicken. I noticed that his face was getting a bit scruffy, and I said something about it.

"Yeah, I know you like beards," he said.

He made a beautiful and amazing meal while I put together the hors d'ouvres, greeted guests and poured the wine. Everyone loved him. He was talkative, asking each guest about what they did and how they knew me. It was evident that he was both a very great man and very smitten with me.

Once everyone had left, he stayed to watch a movie. I was pleased. During the movie, he kissed me. It had been such an amazing night and it became clear to me, sitting next to him and surrounded by my friends at dinner, that there was really something good between us. He was showing me that he felt the same way.

I was too nervous to hear the truth from Kellie and Sophie's mouths about what they thought of Blake, even though I felt like dinner went really well. Sophie called the next day while I was packing up at the house.

"So," she said after a few minutes of small talk. "Jerod and I really liked Blake."

"Really!? Oh, I'm so glad. I was scared to ask!"

"Yeah. We aren't sure about his maturity level, but he's intelligent and we were impressed."

I was so happy. Blake had really liked all of my friends too. He said he'd much rather have dinner and wine with these kinds of friends than be out in the middle of the night getting plastered with his old friends. This was moving in the right direction.

Things went on pretty much like that. He came to bonfires with me. We had a picnic on my living room floor, having been rained out from picnicking in the park, where we had been playing Mexican Train Dominos while he took pictures of me on his phone. Once his leg was mostly healed, I bought a silver bike at the Salvation Army, and we rode our bikes through the park in my neighborhood to the coffee shop on Saturday mornings. I got a library card and we borrowed movies from the library and cooked dinner in my kitchen. Well, he would cook and I would eat pear slices and *Parmesano* cheese and watch him cook. One night, I dreamed that Chase and Blake were step-brothers.

SIXTEEN – THE SKY HAS GOOD INTENTIONS

Every now and then, we'd make plans and then I wouldn't hear from him. Plans for a 9:00 movie night would pass and I would hear from him the following evening. He'd apologize that he was in a fight with his brother and he couldn't call or he's wrecked his bike and he didn't make it home till too late.

I proceeded cautiously. I liked him and I saw something in him. I felt drawn to him enough not to let it go. I believed he was capable of carrying on a successful relationship but I also knew that he was capable of the opposite. By now I was a survivor. I knew how to prepare for the worst and hope for the best.

I casually invited him on a trip home to Westville with me. I knew he would want to get out of his mom's place for a few days, and he wasn't working again yet so he agreed to come. I was protecting my heart well, which was a new habit for me, so I didn't believe that he was really going to come until he got into my car with his backpack.

Blake drove much of the way and we arrived at Meredith's house just in time for dinner. Her family loved him right away. Meredith and her mom were telling me how cute he was as soon as they had a private moment to do so. I knew he was and I couldn't believe that he was there with me, that he felt lucky to be there with me. He told me that when we first met, he had said to a friend about me: "If I get that girl's number I will never ask another girl for her number again."

Cuddled up on an air mattress in the basement, the moon shone through a little window high on the wall. "You look insanely beautiful right now," he whispered and kissed me.

We had decided to do no more than kiss; we wanted to take our time, wanted this to really mean something. We were always intertwined though—awake or asleep. We couldn't stop touching and I loved it.

I let him sleep in the morning while I went to a friend's bridal shower, and when I got back, Blake and Meredith were ready and waiting for me. The three of us went to a wine tasting event at a local winery before heading to the playground on the lake where Meredith and I played growing up.

It was cold at the playground but we had so much fun climbing and swinging from the monkey bars and jumping on the old rubber tires, warmed a little still from the wine. Meredith snapped a picture of Blake and me up on the bridge, arms around each other and smiling at each other blissfully.

It had been my favorite trip home since I moved away almost nine years earlier. As we drove back to Nashville, I

SIXTEEN – THE SKY HAS GOOD INTENTIONS

played my new *Kings of Leon* CD on the stereo and we both sang along.

> *You know that I could use somebody,*
> *Someone like you.*

I wish that was the end of this story, but then again I never did like fairy tales.

April, 2009.

Blake asked me to be his girlfriend officially on the day before Sophie's birthday. I had just run a half marathon, and he came over to teach me how to make mojitos for Sophie's party the next day.

"So, I met these people at the show today," he told me, as he muddled mint leaves in a glass. He stopped and put his arms around my waist and pulled me to him. "And they were talking about dating and sex and stuff, and they asked what my situation was, and I said 'I have a girlfriend and I'm happy about it.'"

"Oh," I said, smiling but trying not to be too dramatic. "Okay."

We had fun at Sophie's birthday. I let Blake ride my scooter and we were all happy from mojitos and celebration. It was one of those nights when things feel as if they'd fallen into place. It was effortless. My friends felt like his friends. My heart felt like it was safely in his hands. Our story felt like it had a happily ever after.

We left Sophie and Jerod's and walked back to my apartment, enjoying the silence and in awe of the multitude of stars in the inky sky. He was mine and I was his, and the night felt like it marked the beginning of everything.

May, 2009.

We knew things would change when he started his new job the next week, helping to open a new restaurant. I knew he would be busy getting things ready and working long hours, but then I didn't hear from him at all for several days. *He could have at least called,* I thought.

That weekend, I finally had a chance to see him. I tried to believe that he was making the best effort that he could. I knew that doing well at this job and finding a place to live that wasn't his mother's house should be his priorities, and I was supportive and patient.

But the more time that passed, the less that I saw him and the less he seemed to care. The month was very back

SIXTEEN – THE SKY HAS GOOD INTENTIONS

and forth: I was okay then I was anxious. I understood then I was livid. He was sorry then he didn't do any better. I hoped that this was temporary, however, by then, I knew in my gut that it wasn't and I was right; he flat out stopped calling.

Somewhere between "Someone Like You" and forever, I'd lost him.

But this time, I didn't lose myself.

I started going back to the pizza place where I hadn't been since the night Chad chose me, fleetingly, over "Jay." I ordered pizza with green peppers and ranch dressing every time. I called it ex-boyfriend pizza. Maybe I should have ordered a large pizza with everything and named one topping for every ex-boyfriend but little nods to Blake and Chad entertained me well enough.

I was more disappointed about the demise of my fledgling relationship with Blake than anything else I'd had lately, but I didn't know him well enough to cry about it and I started hearing things about him that would have concerned me. He got fired for one. I also heard that he had a habit of going through a lot of women the way he went through me.

There was a guy from my group of friends at church who was a guitar tech for a band on tour and we went out a few times during the fall, but we ended up just being friends.

I also went out with a guy who worked in sales for a major computer company and was in a band, but he had been seeing another girl and decided to pursue an exclusive relationship with her. After all, he had been seeing her first and had "invested a lot of time and emotion" into that relationship already as he explained to me more times than necessary.

Despite these quickly fizzling relationships, and despite the fact that I still found myself investing more than I should, I was moving on faster and keeping the focus on everything else that I had going on in my life. I didn't claim to have loved any of them, but I did believe that I could have loved and married each of them if I had been given the chance. With the guitar tech, I thought, "Of course, I always knew I'd end up with a guy who tours." With the salesman, I mentally decorated the townhome he owned, imagining furniture that would compliment his Tuscan Gold walls.

But don't most girls do these things?

Twenty-Seven

November, 2009.

I turned twenty-seven that fall, and to celebrate, I invited everyone that I knew who I felt I would be carrying into the future with me. Anna and her boyfriend, Sophie and Jerod, Kellie, Ben, Liv, friends from church, from styling and from the marketing office, my dance buddy, and even Paul, who had known me through everything. I made a reservation for twenty at a Mexican restaurant and put on a coral colored dress, curled my blonde hair, applied an extra coat of mascara and headed to the restaurant. By the time I got there, the table was already full and the waiters were adding chairs to accommodate more people.

I sat and ordered a margarita, accepted hugs and happy birthday wishes, and then looked from face to face as friends, new and old, all talked and laughed together. It wasn't just the table that was full. It was my life that was full. I was happy with my friends and my career, my home and my hobbies, my relationship with God and my church community, and the way that I was taking good care of myself. I couldn't help but remember my tragic birthday - could that really have been seven years ago? - when no one came at all, and thought about how far I'd come.

When Chase died, my easy belief in true love and soul mates was shaken. When Chad left me, the ability to feel secure and trusting was torn from me. All the guys who didn't see the "me" that I believed I was, or wanted to be, caused me to doubt what I was capable of. It isn't because of these devastations or let downs that I am now, finally, no worse for the wear when those kinds of thing happen. It's because I pushed through them. It's because I did not allow other broken people to break me. I held tightly to the faith that I would someday be a woman of character, strength, and grace, and that people would see that in me. I hoped that she would be loved.

And I am.

Most importantly by one person in particular.

Me.

ACKNOWLEDGEMENTS:

Extra special thanks need to be doled out to so many amazing people. I don't know how I came to be surrounded by the wonderful people I have, but I'll take it!

Coach Evy: You brought so much spice to this story! Thank you for asking the tough questions and helping me to be brave enough to use the answers. I'm proud to call you a friend. To my family: Mom, Dad, Keith, Grandma and all my aunts, uncles and cousins: Thank you for your love and acceptance, and your humor. We all laugh at each other enough that I had no choice but to learn to laugh at myself. Lindsay: You share so much with me! Your time, your home, your children, your words and your heart - and all are so special to me. Krista: From that summer on the soccer fields to our visits now, you always support me and make an effort to be a part of my life, no matter where life takes us. Superglue! Jeremy Westby: You've believed in me and in this story since before a single word lay on a single page. Thank you for being a part of *my* story. The Perdue family: Thank you for "adopting" me and allowing me to be an honorary Perdue! I couldn't ask for a better Nashville family. Carrie and Heather, I love you more than a novel full of words could say.

To everyone else who has cheered me on as I wrote and wrote and wrote, not knowing what this might become. Thank you for saying, "you can do it!" in your own ways. You know who you are!

To everyone who inspired this story, good and bad: Thank you for shaping my heart. I wouldn't be me without you.

Made in the USA
Lexington, KY
08 December 2012